12/12/93

W9-CGN-894

DEKOK AND THE SOMBER NUDE

Books by A.C. Baantjer:
    DeKok and the Somber Nude
    DeKok and the Sunday Strangler
    DeKok and the Corpse on Christmas Eve
    DeKok and the Sorrowing Tomcat
    DeKok and the Disillusioned Corpse
    DeKok and the Romantic Murder
    DeKok and the Dead Harlequin
    DeKok and the Dying Stroller
    DeKok and the Dancing Death
    DeKok and the Corpse on the Church Wall
    DeKok and the Careful Killer
    DeKok and the Naked Lady
    DeKok and the Brothers of the Easy Death
    DeKok and the Deadly Accord
    DeKok and the Murder in Seance
    DeKok and the Begging Death
    DeKok and the Geese of Death
    DeKok and the Dead Lovers
    DeKok and the Mask of Death
    DeKok and the Deadly Warning
    DeKok and the Vendetta
    DeKok and Murder in Ecstacy
    DeKok and Murder by Melody
    DeKok and Death of a Clown
    DeKok and Variations on Murder
    DeKok and Murder by Installments
    DeKok and Murder on Blood Mountain
    DeKok and Corpse by Return
    DeKok and Murder in Bronze
    DeKok and Murder First Class
    DeKok and Murder on the Menu

The Murder of Anna Bentveld
A Loss for Bobby
Thirteen Cats
From the Life of an Amsterdam Constable
and more

DeKok
and the
Somber Nude

by

BAANTJER

translated from the Dutch by H.G. Smittenaar

NEW AMSTERDAM PUBLISHING, Inc.

ISBN 1 881164 01 2

DEKOK AND THE SOMBER NUDE. English translation copyright © 1992 by New Amsterdam Publishing, Inc. Translated from *De Cock en het sombere naakt*, by Baantjer [Albert Cornelis Baantjer], copyright © 1974 and 1978 by Uitgeverij De Fontein, Baarn, Netherlands. All rights reserved. Printed in the United States of America. No part of this book may be used or reproduced in any manner whatsoever without written permission except in the case of brief quotations embodied in critical articles or reviews. For information address New Amsterdam Publishing, Inc., 11205 Bellmont Drive, Fairfax, Virginia, 22030.

Printing History:
    1st Dutch printing: 1967
    2nd Dutch printing: January, 1979
    3rd Dutch printing: December, 1979
    4th Dutch printing: May, 1982
    5th Dutch printing: June, 1984
    6th Dutch printing: April, 1987
    7th Dutch printing: January, 1989
    8th Dutch printing: October, 1990
    9th Dutch printing: September, 1991

    1st American edition: 1992

Cover Design: Studio Combo (Netherlands)
Cover Painting: Judy Sardella
Typography: Monica S. Rozier

DeKok
and the
Somber Nude

1

It was raining. It had been raining for days, endless long July days. Fat, heavy raindrops splashed down from an even gray sky. Insistent, without let-up.

DeKok felt sad and melancholy. His mood was as sensitive as the most precise barometer. A long depression in the weather found its counterpart in him. It affected him like mold.

With his big nose flattened against the window he surveyed the surroundings of the almost legendary, old police station on Warmoes Street in Amsterdam, at the edge of the notorious Red Light District. The rain veiled the nearby rooftops in a curtain of mist and water.

DeKok pressed his lips together. Deep creases appeared at the corners of his mouth. How often had he stood here, lost in thought, struggling with the problems posed by crimes and those who committed them. It had turned him into a gray old man. His upper body had acquired a distinct bow, his shoulders sagged. He thought about it, not with bitterness, but with the mild acceptance with which he was accustomed to look at life in general. Young Vledder, his assistant and understudy, came to join him at the window.

"A good thing," he said contentedly, "that we have no important cases to investigate at the moment. I wouldn't look forward to going out in this type of weather. Brrr . . . no. It's raining cats and dogs!"

"Well," nodded DeKok, "after all, we're in the middle of the dog days." His broad, coarse face with the friendly look of a mild mannered boxer, became serious. He hesitated, then he said: "I remember my old Mother. She didn't like this time of year. You see, the old lady . . . she was a bit superstitious. She never failed to warn me: 'Careful, my boy,' she used to say, 'the dog days of summer can be dangerous.'."

He remained silent and scratched the back of his neck.

"Mother was right. In retrospect, she was always right. She died during the dog days."

DeKok shoved his thick underlip forward and looked up at the gray sky.

"I wouldn't want to die just now," he said after a while.

"What do you mean?" Vledder looked at him in amazement.

DeKok made a lazy and vague gesture toward the heavy, leaden sky. "The heavens are closed," he said somberly.

There was a knock on the door.

Both turned to face the door of the large detective room. There was a light on in the hall outside, although it was the middle of the day. On the frosted glass of the door they observed the shadow of a hooded and cloaked figure. It was a picturesque sight. Again there was a knock on the door.

"Enter," called DeKok.

Slowly the door opened and a young woman appeared in the door opening. She pushed her hood backward and shook out her hair. DeKok estimated her to be in her early twenties. She was beautiful, he noted, extremely beautiful. The long, blonde hair fell in waves over the collar of her black cape. She unhooked the cape and pulled it with an elegant gesture from her slender shoulders. A small shower of fine rain drops cascaded on the floor around her. Vledder hastened to take her cape. She rewarded him with a faint, almost sad, smile. Slowly she entered the bare detective room. As she progressed through the room, the drab institutionalized room seemed to change from gray into a kaleidoscope of colors and sun.

With old-world charm, DeKok offered her a chair next to his desk.

"Please sit down," he said in his most friendly manner.

"Thank you very much."

Carefully she sat down, placed her purse on the edge of the desk and crossed her legs with a mesmerizing gesture. Her movements were slow, refined, aimed at achieving an overwhelming impression.

DeKok looked at her resignedly. The enchantment which had initially conquered him, was quickly replaced by the cool observation of the trained detective. Her manner and movements no longer impressed him. He experienced the alluring scent of her perfume as attractive. No more. He sat down in his chair behind the desk.

"My name is DeKok," he said mildly, "DeKok with . . . eh, kay-oh-kay." he waved in Vledder's direction. "This is my colleague, Inspector Vledder, my right hand. How can we be of service?"

She did not answer at once, hesitated, as if not sure what to say. The hands in her lap moved as if in cramp. The long, narrow fingers worried with the hem of her skirt.

"My name is Kristel, Kristel van Daalen, Van Daalen with double a."

DeKok smiled at her.

"You see, I'm very worried."

"Worried?"

"Yes, very." She sighed deeply.

"Why?"

She looked at him with big, uneasy eyes.

"My cousin has suddenly disappeared."

"Disappeared?"

"Without a trace!" She nodded emphatically.

"Since when?"

"Since yesterday, Mister DeKok. Yesterday, Thursday, she left around three in the afternoon and I haven't seen her since. I went to look in her room when she didn't appear for breakfast and found her bed had not been slept in."

DeKok motioned to Vledder to make notes.

"What's your cousin's name?"

"Nanette, Nanette Bogaard." She paused, gave DeKok a faint smile and added: "Bogaard, with double a."

"Her age?"

"Nineteen. She would have been twenty, next month, in August. We're about two years apart."

The gray sleuth rubbed his hand over his chin. Her manner of speaking affected him.

"Is it usual . . . I mean, did Nanette often stay away from home at night?"

"No. At least, not as far as I know. However, you mustn't think that I watched her all the time. She went her own way. But all night away from home . . . no. In any case, I've never, until now, missed her at breakfast. She was always in time to open the store."

"Store?" DeKok's eyebrows vibrated slightly.

10

"Yes, of course, Nanette and I own a flower shop on old Duke Street. You know, off the Dam, near the New Church, just around the corner from Blue Street. We live there as well, partly behind the store and upstairs. Perhaps you know our store? *Ye Three Roses?*"

"I'm afraid," he answered slowly, "that I'm only familiar with a bar, *The Three Bottles*, on Duke Street."

"I understand," she answered calmly. "Our store isn't that old yet. Uncle Edward died less than two years ago. He liked us a lot, did Uncle Edward. He called us his daisies." She smiled almost shyly. "Nanette and I could always get along very well, you know, even as children. No quarrels . . ." She hesitated and then continued: "When Uncle Edward died, he left us some money. Not a lot, but enough to start the business in Duke Street." She gestured vaguely around her. "We're both from Aalsmeer*, daughters of growers. You know how that goes. You start to think flowers, after a while. Our own flower shop in the middle of Amsterdam, seemed like an ideal, a dream. Uncle Edward's money made it possible to have a dream come true."

She was silent and removed some invisible lint from her skirt.

"We complimented each other beautifully. Nanette is extremely gifted in an artistic way. The pieces she creates are fantastic . . . little jewels. I don't believe that anybody in town can do it better. Our store has, because of the arrangements, gained a certain recognition. The work of Nanette."

DeKok looked at her searchingly.

"And what is your contribution to the enterprise?"

She smiled tiredly.

---

* Aalsmeer: a town in Holland where the growing and exporting of cut flowers is the main industry. Aalsmeer exports approximately $500 million in cut flowers annually, primarily to the USA.

"I'm not artistic. I take care of the business end of the store. I have, what Nanette calls a 'bean-counter soul'. Ach, I'm used to making ends meet, I grew up with it."

It sounded like an apology.

"And Nanette?"

"Nanette wasn't interested in money. She couldn't care less about money."

"What *did* interest her?"

She shrugged her shoulders in a careless gesture.

"Art, literature. All in all she was rather carefree."

The Inspector nodded understanding.

"Perhaps . . .," he said hesitantly, "perhaps, eh, perhaps that's the explanation for her . . . eh, disappearance?"

She looked at him sharply.

"What do you mean?"

"Her carefree attitude. Perhaps there's no reason to worry, perhaps she's just been held up by a friend and perhaps she's just forgotten to give you a call?"

Nervously she pressed her hands together.

"It's really very nice of you," she sighed. "Really, it's very nice that you're trying to allay my fears, but believe me: *something has happened to Nanette!* Something has happened to her. I'm certain."

"You're sure of that?" DeKok looked at her with some intensity.

"Yes."

"Why?"

"Call it female intuition, call it what you want. Laugh at my silly fears, I don't care. I have the inner certainty, that . . ." She remained silent, as if at a loss for words.

Slowly DeKok rose from his chair and walked away from behind his desk. At some distance he stopped, turned and looked at the back of the young woman. His sharp eyes, trained by years of experience, noted every reaction, every minuscule movement of her shoulders.

"Please go on," he said in a compelling voice, "what are you so certain about?"

He saw her swallow.

"Na-Nanette is dead," she stammered.

* * *

A strange silence came over the detective room after Kristel van Daalen's last words.

Vledder looked at DeKok with impatient, questioning eyes. He was not happy with the conversation. A number of questions burned on his tongue. DeKok understood his young colleague. He motioned him to go ahead.

Inspector Vledder was still full of the impetuosity of youth. Purposefully he approached the shrinking figure in the chair, sat himself importantly behind DeKok's desk and cleared his throat with a decisive sound.

DeKok watched from a distance. He liked his younger colleague a lot and he hoped that Vledder would become his successor when he, himself, finally retired.

"Nanette is dead," he heard Vledder say. "At least, that's what you say."

Kristel nodded.

"Yes," she said tonelessly, "Nanette is dead."

"A rather hasty conclusion, if you ask me." His voice sounded hard and penetrating. "There isn't a single clue to point in that direction. That is, you haven't mentioned a single reason for your suspicion."

The young woman raised tearful eyes toward Vledder. A determined expression on her face.

"If you want proof, I can't give it to you, I'm sorry. I mean, I think I have been clear enough. It's just a feeling that Nanette is dead."

She paused and took a deep breath.

"And that is all. It should be enough for you." Her voice sounded reproachful, almost chastising. *"That's all!"* she repeated.

Vledder's face became red.

"Feelings, feelings," he said loudly, "what use are those?"

DeKok interrupted soothingly.

"But that's really everything, isn't it, Miss Van Daalen? Feelings are the basis of our existence."

She gave him a grateful look.

"But you must understand," he continued calmly, "that we need more information about your cousin. If we're to achieve anything at all, at all, we'll need some sort of starting point, some idea as to where, and how, to start our investigations. That's what my colleague meant to say. For instance: Where was Nanette going, yesterday?"

Kristel shrugged her shoulders. "I don't know," she said.

"Did she take a suitcase, or an overnight bag?"

"No, just her purse, no more."

"How was she dressed?"

"Casual, a blue suit."

"Did Nanette have friends?"

"You mean men with whom she associated?"

"Yes."

She made an expansive gesture.

"There were quite a few. Nanette had lots of friends. But recently she used to concentrate mainly on Barry

14

Wielen, a journalist. A nice guy, I must say. Just a little fast, a little too fast for my taste."

DeKok grinned, it was his most attractive feature.

"Journalists live almost constantly at top speed. That's their character. Have you talked to him about Nanette's disappearance?"

"No, I haven't talked about it with anyone. I came straight here."

"All right, then leave everything to us, from now on."

He scratched the back of his neck.

"Oh yes," he asked, "before I forget, do you have a picture of Nanette?"

She opened her purse. After a little searching she found a picture. It was a good, clear picture, roughly postcard size.

"It was taken about a month ago," she said.

DeKok took the picture from her and studied it with care. Nanette Bogaard was a beautiful girl, he saw. She looked a little like her cousin. The same long, blonde hair, the same structure of the face. She was perhaps a little slimmer, more fragile, a Barbie doll come alive. He handed the photo to Vledder.

"You may go home now." DeKok placed a fatherly hand on her shoulder. "As soon as we know something, we'll come and tell you at once."

He walked over to the peg and took her cape.

Slowly the girl rose from her chair. DeKok draped the cape over her shoulders.

"If you find Nanette at home, in a little while, please let us know."

"No, Mr. DeKok, Nanette is dead."

Sadly she shook her head.

2

With his hands deep in his pockets, DeKok paced up and down the Detective room. He mulled over the conversation with Kristel, the words, the intonations, the gestures.

DeKok could do that. He had an almost photographic memory, with a love for detail. A seemingly unimportant slip of the tongue, a facial expression, he noticed it all. He was born with the gift, but his profession had honed the gift to a fine art.

In front of the window, his favorite spot, he halted. It was still raining. Suddenly he turned around and walked over to the peg on the wall.

"Get your coat, my boy. We're off!"

Vledder looked surprised at his boss and teacher.

"Say," he called, suspicion in his voice, "you're not planning to already start looking for Nanette . . . eh . . .?"

"Bogaard," completed DeKok.

"Right, Bogaard. You're not already looking for her, are you? The girl has barely been gone twenty four hours. Surely, there's no reason to panic?"

"Her cousin says she's dead." DeKok looked at him evenly.

"Her cousin is crazy, I tell you, her with her *feelings*, her female intuition. Just because this dizzy flower girl took it in her head to imagine her cousin dead, you want to alert the entire police force?"

DeKok struggled into his old raincoat.

"No," he answered calmly, "not the entire police force, my boy, just the two of us. For the moment that ought to be enough."

Vledder shook his head in desperation. He couldn't understand his old teacher. He didn't see the connection. He walked over to DeKok and placed himself in front of the old sleuth. He raised a finger in the air.

"Just listen to me," he said, irritated. "Young Nanette has never been away from home, overnight, that is, according to her cousin."

"And?"

"But she's nineteen years old, you get it? DeKok, think: nineteen! Just the right age to start experiencing the occasional nightly adventure. What harm can that do? That's healthy."

"I know a lot of fathers," answered DeKok casually, "who would prefer some different sort of healthy activity for their nineteen year old daughters."

Vledder sighed.

"You know quite well what I mean. There's no question of a real missing person. What does Miss Van Daalen want from us? She can hardly expect us to call out the troops every time that a nineteen year old sleeps away from home. That's, that is . . .," Vledder searched for the right word, "that's . . . eh, . . . monk's work!"

"Monk's work?"

"Yes, you know, one letter at a time, year after year, never an end, you know what I mean."

DeKok laughed loudly. He placed his old, decrepit little felt hat on the back of his head and walked out of the room. Vledder, furious, followed. His raincoat bunched up on his shoulders.

* * *

Barry Wielen turned out to be a tall, slender young man with friendly eyes and a moustache of which the points pointed proudly at the sky. DeKok was visibly impressed by the moustache. He looked at it with admiring attention. The young man found this attention for his upper lip growth embarrassing. He moved restlessly under the searching eyes of DeKok.

"What do you want?"

The Inspector shoved his hat a little farther on the back of his head and wiped the rain off his face with a handkerchief.

"That you take these wet raincoats from us."

The young man grinned, embarrassed.

"Of course, of course, I'm sorry."

Suddenly he came in action. He helped divest them of their coats, put them away and led them into a large, spacious room. It was somewhat messy, but clean and cozy.

DeKok cleared an easy chair. Without waiting for an invitation, he sat down and stretched his legs with a groan of pleasure. Vledder followed his example. Wielen watched the performance, at a loss for words, a surprised look on his face.

"What can I do for you, gentlemen?" It sounded a bit timid.

DeKok shaped his face into a friendly grin. It was always a new surprise to Vledder how attractive that made him look. DeKok looked at Wielen from the depths of his easy chair and said:

"Nanette Bogaard."

"What!?"

"Nanette Bogaard," repeated DeKok. "She's still under age* and we're here to fetch her."

"I don't know what you're talking about," said Wielen, a vacant look on his face.

"It's really not all that difficult," said the Inspector. "You asked what we wanted? Well, we're police inspectors, attached to the Warmoes Street Station. We want Nanette Bogaard. According to our information, she's here in the house."

"What!?"

"Your vocabulary is rather limited. You also seem to be rather slow in the comprehension department. Bad character traits for a journalist, I'd say. But, all right, I'll try to be clearer." He lit a cigarette and blew the smoke toward the ceiling in a gesture calculated to annoy.

"Nanette Bogaard, as stated, is an under age girl. We have reasons to believe that she spent last night with you. In case you do not turn her over to us, if you keep her hidden, or if you refuse to cooperate in our investigations, you may be charged with kidnapping." He paused for the desired effect, then he continued: "And kidnapping is, of course, a criminal offense." DeKok made it sound like a special treat.

The journalist looked at him, a dazed look on his face.

"Criminal offense?" he repeated.

"Yes, absolutely, Article 281 of our very own Criminal Code. An interesting article. You should read it sometime. The minimum is six years, no parole."

---

* 21 years is the age of consent in the Netherlands.

"Six years?" Wielen furrowed his brow.

"Yes, a long time. When you're finished you'd be about thirty," nodded DeKok and added: "Almost an old man."

Barry Wielen sat down and rubbed his hand over his eyes. He was trying to gather his thoughts. Normally he was able to control himself, he was able to control the situation. It was something his profession required. But DeKok had given him no time.

He looked into the friendly eyes of the gray detective across from him. The face appeared cunning and irresistible. Slowly Barry got hold of himself, made an attempt to recover. He became alert. The journalist in him took charge of the situation and decided not to knuckle under. A faint smile appeared underneath his gorgeous moustache.

"I wish it were true," he said.

The Inspector looked at him, noted the change in attitude and asked:

"What do you mean?"

"I wish it were true that Nanette had spent the night with me. I must say, it is an exciting idea."

He grinned softly. His face became almost as attractive as that of DeKok when *he* grinned.

"But I'm sorry to have to disappoint you," Wielen continued, "Nanette isn't here. She hasn't been here. Search the premises, if you want. You'll not find her. I haven't seen her for at least two weeks."

"So you do know her?"

"Yes, of course. Nanette, wow-wow-wow, what a woman! A treasure." He laughed with his entire face. "The wild daisy from *Ye Three Roses*."

DeKok pulled up the left side of his mouth. It looked like a snarl.

"Wow-wow-wow," he repeated evenly. It took all feeling out of the expression. "And when," he continued, "was the last time you saw wow-wow-wow Nanette?"

"I told you, about two weeks ago. It was more or less an accidental meeting."

"How, more or less accidental?"

"Well . . . eh," suddenly he stopped. Wielen looked at DeKok. He looked from DeKok to Vledder and back again. A look of utter surprise came over him.

"Something is wrong here." He shook his head and then asked: "Since when would two inspectors from the Warmoes Street be interested in vice? You're Homicide! Why this interest in Nanette?"

"She's gone."

"Who?"

"Nanette."

"Gone?"

DeKok nodded.

"Kristel van Daalen, her cousin from *Ye Three Roses*, reported her missing this morning. Now do you understand our interest?"

Vaguely Wielen nodded.

"Sure, sure," he admitted, absent-minded. Apparently he had some trouble accepting the disappearance of Nanette as fact. "Please go on," he said.

"You spoke of an accidental meeting?"

Wielen leaned forward and reached for a pack of cigarettes on the coffee table. DeKok looked at the long, sinewy fingers of the journalist. They shook.

"Yes, yes, that meeting."

He lit the cigarette and inhaled deeply.

"It was evening. Around half past ten, I think. I'd just left the paper. I had just finished the report of a court case

22

I was assigned to earlier that day. I drove via the Dam and skirted the Red Light District." He gestured with his cigarette. "Suddenly I saw Nanette turn onto High Street, she came from the quarter."

DeKok looked unbelievingly at the journalist.

"Nanette came from the Red Light District?"

"From the District, yes. I too, thought it strange. Really. I didn't know her all that well, but Nanette never struck me as the kind of girl who could be found anywhere near the District. I could hardly believe my eyes."

"What did you do?"

"At first I drove on, then I turned and passed her, coming from behind. I looked in my rear view mirror."

"And?"

"I hadn't been mistaken. It was her. I drove on and parked on the Dam, near the Monument. From there I walked to Duke Street. I waited for her near *Ye Three Roses*. It didn't take long. She arrived shortly after."

"What did she say?"

Again Barry pulled on his cigarette.

"I just did as if I'd met her by chance. I didn't mention that I had seen her come from the District. I didn't really dare mention the subject. You understand, I didn't want to give the impression that I'd been spying on her. After all, I didn't have any right to call her on it. She wasn't exactly responsible to me."

DeKok looked at him searchingly.

"I thought," he said carefully, "I thought . . . that eh, the both of you . . ."

A sad grin spread fleetingly over the face of the young man.

"Ach," he said, "it's really never been more than some slight flirtation, a game to Nanette."

DeKok listened to the tone of voice.

"You're in love with her?"

Again Wielen sighed.

"In love, yes, you could call it that."

"And Nanette?"

Nonchalantly he shrugged his shoulders.

"She was too playful. Not serious enough." He looked at DeKok for a moment. "After all," he concluded, "love is a serious business, don't you agree?"

"Without a doubt," nodded the Inspector. "There have been quite a few murders because of love. Certainly, love is serious enough."

"Murders?" Wielen looked trapped.

"Love is one of the prime reasons for murder."

The journalist brought a hand up to his forehead. The intelligent look in his eyes disappeared. He started to grin like a fool.

"I, eh, I haven't killed Nanette," he almost stuttered.

DeKok reacted quickly: "Who said so?"

"Nobody, nobody, but I thought, I mean . . ."

For a long time DeKok looked at Wielen thoughtfully. Then he rubbed his hand through his gray hair. He had weighed the reactions of the journalist, but his impressions were mixed. "Did Nanette say anything?" he asked.

"When?"

"That night, in front of *Ye Three Roses*?"

"No, nothing. Well, I mean, we chatted awhile. But she didn't tell me where she'd been, that night. She went inside after about half an hour."

"And were you able to solve the puzzle later? I take it that the question of Nanette and the Red Light District occupied you to some extent?"

"Indeed, but I haven't seen her since."

"So that was two weeks ago?"

"Yes, two weeks."

* * *

They remained silent together for a long time. The journalist lit another cigarette, his third. He had barely finished the previous one. Young Wielen was obviously nervous, tense. He could not hide it. There was a hunted look in his eyes, jumpy, like a scared, chased animal. His left hand kept turning the points of his extravagant moustache.

DeKok noticed the tension.

Vledder looked bored. He had listened carefully to the conversation between his old teacher and the journalist. He had made notes. At first he had been interested. Although he was more or less familiar with DeKok's methods, he always enjoyed seeing the old master in action. But now, his interest had become purely professional. Vledder did not believe Nanette had disappeared. As far as he was concerned, the girl had stayed away from home for a night. So what? He thought DeKok made too much fuss over the case. Before long Nanette would reappear and then all this trouble would have been for nothing. The thought made him angry. Dammit, they had better things to do than running after little cousins with an urge for adventure. Slowly DeKok looked around the room. His glance took in the bare walls, absorbed the spare furniture. He stood up, almost lazily, with slow movements.

He had discovered something that did not fit in the somewhat messy, disordered, room of Barry Wielen. It was a lovely dissonant, sunny and full of color. It had pride of place, near the window, on top of a battered bookcase. It soothed DeKok's vision. It was a small bunch of wild flowers, artistically arranged in a thin, pale porcelain vase, decorated with a pink ribbon. A small masterpiece of the art of flower arranging. DeKok walked over to the bookcase and lifted the small vase carefully in his hand. He looked at the flowers with interest. "Gorgeous," he murmured appreciatively, "extremely well done. I have seldom seen anything as fine as this."

After a while he replaced the vase, careful, as if he was handling an important and fragile religious relic. He stood and looked at it for a while longer. His hand supported his chin.

"It's a pity," he sighed, "that wild flowers are so fragile. They don't last long." His voice sounded genuinely depressed.

"It should be a crime. I mean, it should be prohibited to pluck wild flowers. They belong outside, in the fields, the woods, among the corn."

He gestured at Vledder. "How long, do you think, that wild flowers will last, remain fresh and vibrant, in a stuffy bachelor's room?"

Carelessly Vledder shrugged his shoulders. He did not understand the direction, or the purpose, of DeKok's question.

"I don't know," he said hesitantly, "a few days . . . a week, perhaps?"

Thoughtfully DeKok nodded agreement.

"A few days, a week," he repeated. "You're right. Certainly not longer. The slender stems will wilt quickly."

Again he looked at the colorful bouquet, long, carefully and with an admiring look in his eyes. Only after several minutes did he turn away. His face was expressionless, like a mask. He crossed the room and halted in front of the journalist.

"Barry Wielen," he said calmly, "there's but a single person able to arrange some ordinary wild flowers in such a refined and artistic manner . . . your, or let's say our, friend Nanette, the wild daisy from *Ye Three Roses.*"

3

Inspector DeKok raked his short, thick fingers through his stiff, gray hair. It was a habit when he was deep in thought. Lazily, he leaned back in his chair, his relatively short legs on the edge of the desk. Nanette's disappearance had disturbed him. He did not know why, exactly. People disappeared daily. Their tracing was one of the routine jobs assigned to detectives all over the country. Sometimes the people who disappeared were just plain tired, tired of their wives, their husbands. They had had it with their boss, their house, their office, their job, their worries, everything. They just walked away from it all, away from the mind-deadening routine, the constant demands of daily life. A flight, a flight toward freedom. But usually it did not last long. It seemed that freedom, too, had its negative aspects. They soon missed the comfortable protection of their familiar surroundings, the sweet slumber of the daily grind.

Usually the rebellion was played out after a few days and they would return, sometimes disillusioned, awakened, but always painfully apologetic and full of remorse, and again part of the respectable community.

DeKok pressed his lips together.

But Nanette, so it seemed, was different. There was no question of a dissatisfaction with life, no flight from the daily grind. There was something else to cause her sudden disappearance, a different motive. But what?

It was all still so unclear, he thought, so vague, so indefinite. There were no logical conclusions to be drawn, no matter how hard one tried.

He took his legs off the desk and produced a large sheet of paper from a drawer.

HOW OR WHY OR THROUGH WHOM DID NANETTE DISAPPEAR?

He wrote it with big letters at the top of the page. It was as if the thought so occupied him, that he needed to see it in front of him, as a sort of challenge to his imagination. He sighed, put the pen down and looked at the question. Was it fear?

Vledder sat at his own desk, a little distance away, and worked on his notes. He still did not understand DeKok's interest in the disappearance of Nanette Bogaard. It was usual to wait a few days before investigations were started. That was the usual procedure. Experience had shown, over and over again, that it was virtually useless to panic right away when a person had disappeared. DeKok should know that. He was an old campaigner. How long had he been on the job, so far? Twenty, twenty five years? At least. He had become gray in the job.

Vledder rose from behind his desk and walked toward DeKok. Despite everything, he genuinely liked his old teacher. It was a deep affection that had its origin in loyalty and admiration.

"Wow-wow-wow," he laughed.

Annoyed, DeKok looked up.

"Wow-wow-wow," repeated Vledder.

DeKok grinned disdainfully.

"It's a constant marvel to me," he said, "that the clear sounds of our beautiful language are constantly being improved." He snorted. "Heaven knows what the exact meaning of that primitive utterance may be."

Vledder laughed.

"Well, you see, when a stallion spots a good looking filly, it starts to neigh ..."

"I understand," answered DeKok. His tone was disapproving. "... and when a civilized young man spots a beautiful girl, he too, relieves his feelings by uttering animal sounds."

"That's it. It's the modern way." Vledder remained silent for a while, then he continued: "But even without the, to you, strange 'wow-wow-wow', I amused myself immensely at the home of Barry Wielen. It was really funny. Wielen was as slippery as an eel. You should go on the stage. He knew what you meant with your comedy about the wild flowers. But he also knew that you had not one iota of proof."

Nonchalant, DeKok shrugged his shoulders.

"But our friend is lying, all the same. You see, the little act of mine, with the wild flowers, wasn't just a game. Of course, there's no legal evidence, I mean, nothing you could take to court, but it was an indication, to me, that Wielen has visited his friend Nanette in *Ye Three Roses*, not too long ago."

"How long ago?"

"In any case, less than two weeks ago. That arrangement couldn't have been put together long, maybe a day or so."

Vledder nodded, then said: "But perhaps he's been in *Ye Three Roses*, but didn't see Nanette ... ?"

31

"Of course, that's possible. But I have the feeling that Wielen is hiding something, that he knows more than he's telling us."

Vledder grabbed a chair and sat down on it backward, his arms folded on the backrest.

"What do you think? Should we have him followed?"

"Waste of time." DeKok shook his head. "That's hardly necessary with a reporter."

A look of incomprehension fled briefly across Vledder's face. "Not necessary? he asked. "But if he . . ."

"Take it from me," interrupted DeKok, "The print-press-boys are never very clever, or cunning, they're merely bold and ill-advised."

He grimaced.

"Our old Commissaris always used to say: 'Give a reporter enough rope and sooner or later he'll hang himself.' Did you ever hear of him?" There was nostalgia in DeKok's voice. "After all," he continued, "it's in the very character of a reporter. He can't fight it. Give him time and before long, he'll publicize anything."

"Even his confession?"

"Perhaps," grinned DeKok, "it all depends on the size of the headline he thinks he'll get."

Vledder laughed.

"What about his story about the District? Do you really believe he saw Nanette come from the Red Light District?"

DeKok scratched the back of neck.

"I don't know," he hesitated. "he was rather glib with that story. He didn't need any prompting. That surprised me a bit, you know. I wonder if it could be a trap."

"A trap?"

---

* Commissaris: A rank equivalent to Captain..

"Yes, perhaps Wielen wants us to look for the cause of Nanette's disappearance in the area of the District, while ..."

"... while the District has nothing to do with her disappearance," completed Vledder. Then he grinned and added: "The little whores are as innocent as the driven snow."

DeKok nodded approval, while managing to show disapproval for Vledder's choice of words.

"But then," continued Vledder, "Wielen may be more cunning than you're trying to make me believe."

DeKok smiled faintly. He placed both hands on the desk and pressed his heavy upper body into a standing position.

"I've a little job for you," he said.

Vledder's eyes sparkled.

"You want me to track the reporter, after all?"

"Just leave Wielen be. That can wait. I want you to go to Aalsmeer. Just ask around at the police station, there, and have a little chat with Nanette's parents."

"You want me to tell them that ...?"

"No, not yet. Just try to find out if the relationship between the two cousins is really as idyllic as Kristel led us to believe. Perhaps they know more about it in Aalsmeer."

Vledder nodded. His face was serious.

"And what are you going to do? he asked.

"I, I'm going to Lowee."

DeKok grinned broadly. He never looked more attractive.

* * *

Lowee, was better known in the Red Light District as "Little" Lowee, for obvious reasons. He had a small body, a narrow chest and a mouse face. Little Lowee and DeKok had known each other for years. Based on a broad interpretation of mutual respect, one could even speak of a certain liking for each other. Yes, they liked each other, DeKok and Little Lowee, but a real friendship had never developed. That was impossible. A barrier always remained, a nebulous veil of suspicious alertness. It was a wall that could not be torn down. After all, DeKok was a cop, a representative of the Law, a man of authority. Little Lowee was a petty criminal. There were no two ways about it, worlds separated them. Near the Station, on the edge of the District, at the corner of the Barn Alley, was the small, intimate bar of Little Lowee. The bar, with its shadowy, slightly pink interior was the meeting place for the girls of the Quarter. This is where they rested, Black Tracies and Blonde Gretas, here they sipped their sweet concoctions and chatted openly about their business. The hookers without a regular boy friend looked here, motivated by a need for love, for a good looking partner, a real man with an excess of virility, because in the routine of their business there was little excitement. And a person wants, needs, some of that, from time to time. Little Lowee knew. Little Lowee knew everything. The Quarter had no secrets for Little Lowee.

* * *

DeKok shuffled to the end of the bar and hoisted himself on a bar stool. It was his regular place. From there he could look over the entire room and his back was covered in case of unexpected eventualities, such as the spontaneous fights between two sisters in the world's oldest profession. Because competition is rife in any business.

Little Lowee came over to DeKok's part of the bar and placed a glass in front of the detective. His other hand felt under the bar for the bottle of Napoleon Cognac, never wasted on his regular customers, but which was reserved exclusively for DeKok. It was a gesture of respect for the gray sleuth.

"How's crime?" asked Lowee pleasantly, while he poured generously.

"Everybody has got a cross to bear," grimaced DeKok. "My cross is the sins of others."

Little Lowee smiled with a crooked mouth.

"If I didn't know you better," he jeered, "I'd be getting tears in my eyes." He poured a generous measure for himself from the same bottle and raised his glass to DeKok.

"*Proost*, to all children of thirsty fathers."

DeKok grinned: "*Proost!*" he answered.

He rocked the glass slightly in his hands and inhaled the tantalizing aroma of the cognac. DeKok was a connoisseur. He took another small sip and enjoyed the sensation of beneficial inner warmth the liquor seemed to spread through his body. It banished the wet chill of the rain. Carefully he replaced the snifter on the bar.

"I'm looking for a girl."

Half surprised, Little Lowee looked at him.

"I'd have thought you would be far past it, by now," he grinned softly.

DeKok ignored the remark. He took Nanette's picture from an inside pocket and placed it in front of the bar owner.

"This is the one."

Little Lowee wiped his hands on the front of his shirt and picked up the photo. He looked at it with care.

"Good looking broad," he said finally, admiration in his voice. He pressed his lower lip forward, nodded his head emphatically and repeated: "Very good looking broad."

DeKok nodded agreement.

"Do you know her?" he asked.

Little Lowee did not answer at once. He wiped the back of his hand over his mouth.

"She's supposed to be in business, here?"

DeKok shrugged his shoulders.

"To be honest, I don't know. She seems a nice girl. It has been said that she visits the neighborhood from time to time. But if you ask me, she doesn't belong."

"There's a lot of women that don't belong here," snorted Lowee.

DeKok was aware of the correction. Little Lowee was rather touchy on that subject. As were most of the people who made a living from the underbelly of society. They didn't like "nice" people. As they often knew so well, "nice" was just a facade, a camouflage, to hide behind. They saw too many so-called "nice" and "respectable" people in the District. They were not all tourists.

"I know what you mean," sighed DeKok.

Lowee sipped his cognac.

"What's she done?" he asked casually.

DeKok smiled.

"No, no, it isn't that. The girl is gone, just gone. Disappeared without a trace. She's underage. A family member reported her missing."

Little Lowee's small, lively face cleared up. The subject "disappeared underage girl" was a "safe" subject in the neighborhood. It could freely be discussed with the police. The Quarter was not supposed to be a haven for underage runaways. That was the unwritten code of the Red Light District.

"How old is she, exactly?"

"Nineteen."

"And you gotta find her?" sniggered Lowee.

"What do you expect, it's my profession."

"So, and whadda we call this flower?"

"Nanette, Nanette Bogaard."

"What did you say?"

"Nanette Bogaard."

Little Lowee put his glass down and thought deeply. It was obvious. His face was distorted, as if in pain. Thinking could be a painful experience for Little Lowee.

"Bogaard . . . Bogaard," he said thoughtfully, "I think I may have heard that moniker once or twicet."

DeKok sat up straight.

"Are you sure?" his voice was hopeful.

Lowee nodded vaguely.

"I woulda been very wrong, if I said otherwise." His lower lip curled itself upward.

"Bogaard, you see, it's rather a strange name, around here, you must remember that."

With difficulty DeKok controlled his impatience.

"Where did you hear the name?"

"I think it was right here, in the bar."

"A business girl?"

Lowee shook his head.

"No, not a woman, a guy, I shoulda said."

"A guy, what sort of guy?"

Little Lowee pulled a face, as if in disgust.

"Ach, you know, a guy, one of those dirty stargazers, capable of anything. He comes around a bit, I think, lately."

"I never heard of him."

"That's possible, he ain't been part of the scene for long."

He looked at DeKok and grinned. "Somehow I don't think that he'd be especially dying to meet you."

DeKok shrugged his shoulders and drained his glass.

"Still, I would like to talk to him."

Lowee poured again.

"About the broad?"

"Yes, I find the similarity of names a bit too coincidental, too obvious. Perhaps he knows something."

The small barkeeper nodded.

"I just don't think it'll be easy to catch up to him. He's rather a shy sorta guy, I've been told."

DeKok bestowed his sunniest smile upon the small man.

"Perhaps . . . maybe, if you gave him a little hint . . ."

"A hint?

"Yes, you know, a friendly invitation, an appointment for . . ." DeKok looked at his watch. ". . . for, let's say, tonight at eight. Tell him to go to 48, Warmoes Street, room nine."

"The station?"

"Yes."

A petite black girl, rather provocatively dressed, emerged from between the leather curtains that separated the bar from the minuscule lobby. A young man with dark glasses and dirty blonde hair, followed close behind. Little Lowee looked over his shoulder. Through the large mirror behind the bar he followed the couple with his eyes. They sat down at a small table in the back. Lowee turned back to DeKok, a tic had developed near his left eye.

"I . . . eh, I'd rather not," he said hesitantly.

DeKok rubbed his face with his hand.

"And I thought we were friends," it sounded reproach-ful. "I mean, such a small service isn't too much to ask, now, is it?"

Lowee heard the disappointment and squirmed. His face assumed the usual painful expression. Obviously he was on the horns of a dilemma. A drop of sweat emerged from under his sparse hair and rolled down his forehead. He was uncomfortable. DeKok looked at him in amazement.

"Well, what's your answer?" he pressed. "Will you do it?"

Little Lowee leaned confidentially closer to DeKok.

"Why," he whispered, "why don't you ask him yourself?"

DeKok's eyebrows started to vibrate.

"Myself?"

Almost imperceptibly, Little Lowee nodded.

"He just came in."

4

DeKok, cognac glass in one hand, slid off the bar stool. Almost strolling, the decrepit little felt hat shoved onto the back of his head, he waddled through the pinkish twilight of Little Lowee's cafe. He looked like a jolly drunk in his fifties, filled with the indestructible belief that the sole purpose of mankind was to be drunk, jolly and cozy at all times. In the far corner, near the table of the young couple, he halted. The conversation between the two young people stopped immediately. DeKok smiled his best smile and without invitation allowed himself to sit down on the vacant chair next to the black girl. She moved slightly aside, demonstratively, as if he was infected.

DeKok placed his cognac glass in front of him. After carefully placing both elbows on the edge of the small table, he rested his head on the entwined fingers of his hands and stared at the young man in front of him. His sharp gaze seemed to touch the face. The dark glasses hid some of the features. But a slight vibration around the corners of the mouth betrayed the fact that the young man was less than pleased with the scrutiny.

"Get away," he hissed between his teeth, "we didn't call you."

DeKok took a careful sip of his cognac and played with the glass in his hand.

"I often come without being called," he said in a sepulcher tone of voice. "I'm like Death. It's an element of surprise."

The young man hesitated. The tone of voice was not that of a drunk. It confused him.

"Well, we, we don't wish to be disturbed," he explained. "You understand?"

DeKok nodded.

"I understand," he said with a friendly note in his voice. "Therefore, I won't keep you long. But in case you're interested, my name is DeKok. DeKok with . . . eh, kay-oh-kay. I'm an inspector assigned to the station in the Warmoes Street, Homicide." He paused, then continued: ". . . as part of my duties, I'm involved in the investigations regarding the mysterious disappearance of Nanette Bogaard."

"Nanette?" The young man was visibly shocked.

DeKok nodded.

"Nanette Bogaard," he emphasized.

The young man swallowed, his adam's apple moved up and down.

"Disappeared?" he asked.

"Yes, are you interested?" DeKok looked at him sharply.

The young man threw a hunted look in the direction of his black companion.

"Well, yes, no, not interested, not really, actually," he stammered. He motioned vaguely and nervously and tried to force a smile that did not succeed. "Actually, it's not all that peculiar. I'm sure that girls disappear all the time."

Slowly DeKok rose.

"Yes," he answered somberly, "Yes, and sometimes they disappear forever."

He pushed his chair back, preparatory to leaving. It was an awkward movement, as if he was not too steady on his legs. Suddenly he lost his balance. He fell diagonally across the table. The empty cognac glass was knocked over. A slight noise built up in the room. DeKok stayed where he was. When he finally moved again, his hand, as if by accident, touched the dark glasses. Momentarily they revealed the eyes hidden behind. It was just a moment, a flash of insight, but it was enough for DeKok. He laughed, a bit embarrassed, murmured an apology and waddled outside.

The couple looked after him with mixed emotions.

Little Lowee grinned from behind the bar.

* * *

As soon as the brown, leather reinforced curtains of Lowee's bar closed behind DeKok, he tightened the belt of his raincoat some more, put up the collar and shoved his little, ridiculous hat a bit further over his eyes. Slowly he walked away from the bar. It was still raining. Lost tourists, draped in wrinkled plastic, paraded along the windows of the District. A sad amusement. DeKok looked at the wet, curious faces. Amsterdam in July. Sightseeing boats, their windows fogged over, moved through the canals.

At the end of the canal he stopped, undecided. He thought about returning to the station and to request a nationwide search for the missing girl. So far he had resisted the urge. He felt it was a bit early, a bit precipitous. But he was more and more convinced that something serious had happened. He had known it all along. Almost from the moment that Kristel had uttered the name of her cousin. He could not explain it. There was no rational explanation. It was just a strange feeling of disaster, death, mystery. An uncanny premonition, irrational, but usually accurate. There were a number of logical explanations for Nanette's disappearance, but that did nothing to alleviate his feelings, his fears. They remained in his subconscious, irresistible, like malevolent phantoms.

A cold drop of rain slid down the bridge of his nose. It reminded him that it was pretty unproductive to stand on a street corner, especially in the rain. He cursed himself. Before long the wet would creep into his bones and he would have another cold. He was much too susceptible for the Dutch climate. His indecision was in the process of killing every possible initiative. He had to do something.

Upon further deliberation, he decided to wait a little longer with an APB. There was still time for that. Perhaps young Vledder had discovered something in Aalsmeer that would give the case a totally different direction. One never knew. An investigation involving a lively young girl was always full of surprises. Lively? Suddenly an idea crossed his mind. Lively? ... *how* lively was Nanette Bogaard? Was it possible that the lack of liveliness was the cause of her disappearance? Melancholy, sorrow, suicide? DeKok pressed his wet hat a little deeper into his forehead and walked in the direction of Duke Street. Kristel van Daalen, he thought, had to know something more.

Ye Three Roses, it appeared, was an exclusive flower shop with an artistic interior, exotic flowers and fantastic prices. The careful, bureaucratic soul of DeKok decided never to send flowers to his wife from this particular location. Not because he did not wish his wife to have the best of everything. But, so thought DeKok, there are, after all, limits.

The 'ding-dong' of the store bell had long since wafted away into silence before Kristel van Daalen appeared from behind a flagstone counter. Her appearance coincided with the soft whispering of bamboo curtains. DeKok looked up. Again he experienced the attraction of her extraordinary beauty. She looked adorable in a light blue duster.

She approached him with a friendly smile and offered her hand. Her long, almost sinewy fingers closed around his hand. DeKok was surprised at the strong, unfeminine strength of her grip, so in contrast with the rest of her appearance.

"Well, Mr. DeKok," she asked, "Have you found a trace of Nanette?" Her voice sounded gaily hopeful.

Sadly, DeKok shook his head.

"No," he said apologetically, "No, I don't know a thing, yet. Of course, we're trying, you understand. But so far we've had very little luck."

She nodded thoughtfully.

"It *is* strange, so sudden like. You can't help but wonder what has happened to her."

DeKok removed his hat and unbuttoned his coat.

"Do you have any suggestions?"

"Not a one."

She shrugged her shoulders in a helpless gesture.

DeKok pointed at the wet store front.

"I could imagine," he said, "that this kind of weather might want to make somebody suddenly long for another land, a different climate, a southern location, full of warmth and sun-drenched beaches."

She disciplined a rebellious lock of blond hair with the back of her hand.

"You mean that Nanette . . .?"

"It's only a suggestion."

"Do you find it plausible?" She smiled.

"Well, I just try to apply my own feelings, druthers, if you like, to the situation. Whenever I see the window of a Travel Agency, full of posters about warm climes, laughing people in the sun, I always have the urge to just walk away from it all, to go there. Leave it all behind." He grinned self-consciously. "But, at my age, you always think about the consequences of such a bold step. And the consequences are always too many, much too many."

"And if you were younger?" She looked at him with interest.

DeKok grinned.

"How young? Nanette's age?"

Kristel did not answer. She glanced away and looked at the electric clock on the wall. She stared at it, without seeing anything for a while. It was three minutes to six.

"I'll close up for the day," she decided. "It's almost that time, anyway. I don't expect any more customers at this hour." She gave him a friendly smile.

"Perhaps you'd like to come in for a while?" she asked.

"Yes," nodded DeKok, "I'd like to see her room, anyway."

"Her room?"

"Yes, where she slept. Perhaps there are letters, or other papers, which can help give us a starting point. Some young women keep a diary."

He noticed she was visible upset at the thought.

"A diary?"

DeKok nodded. His face was serious.

"Not so often anymore. But it happens. Especially dreamy girls, those with a romantic inclinations, feel the

46

need to entrust their more intimate thoughts to the pages of a diary. Some consider it a sort of confession."

"Confession?"

"Yes, a written declaration. It's very interesting literature. Sometimes it reveals the most surprising thoughts and disclosures."

DeKok made a tired gesture, then continued: "Usually they're very secretive about it and take good care of it. I mean, they're not easy to find, these diaries. They're sometimes hidden in the strangest places."

She wrinkled her nose and snorted audibly.

"Silly," she said. "Childish."

The irritated tone did not escape DeKok.

"You never kept a diary?" he asked.

It was a superfluous question and DeKok knew it.

She looked at him as if he was an enemy.

"I never," her voice sounded irked, "had time for such foolishness."

"And Nanette?"

She walked to the front door.

"I don't know," she remarked in passing, "I never paid any attention."

Carefully she closed the door. Two bolts and a Yale lock. Then she shut off a number of hidden light sources. Suddenly it was dark in the store. All color had disappeared.

"Are you coming?" she asked.

She disappeared behind the counter and through the bamboo curtain. Almost reluctantly, DeKok followed the scent of her perfume. The scent excited him for a moment, a very short moment.

She led him to a short, narrow corridor. A few brass hooks were attached to one wall and served as clothing hooks.

"You can get rid of your coat here," she said and disappeared.

DeKok found a place for his old, but much loved hat and took off his raincoat. He quickly moved his hand over the shoulders and back of his jacket. It felt wet. He cursed quietly to himself. His raincoat had soaked through again. It was his own fault. His wife had told him, time and again, to get rid of the old coat and to buy a new one. But DeKok did not like new things, he was attached to the old raincoat. Almost as much as to his old, decrepit hat.

An oval mirror, in a frame of Scottish plaid, was placed next to the brass hooks. Mirrors were always too low for DeKok. He bent forward and looked at his reflection in the mirror. It seemed to cheer him up. He always felt that his face was a bit ridiculous and could never understand why others would take him seriously, at times. After all, with such a face . . . He smiled at himself, adjusted his tie and walked toward the door of the room. He stopped short in the doorway. It was as if everything had become less visible. There seemed to be a fog in front of his eyes, a magical veil of whispering taffeta and lace.

He rubbed the back of his hands over his eyes . . . tried to focus. She stood in the middle of the room, smiling, inviting in a tight fitting dress that left little to the imagination and served as a witness to her beauty.

DeKok took a deep breath and succeeded in dispersing the enchantment. He wondered what exactly had tricked him, what had veiled his clear observation. He analyzed. It had been her smile, he decided, and her look full of sweet promises. It had been the cause of a slightly increased heartbeat and additional flow of blood to the head. Embarrassed, he scratched the back of his neck and banished his foolishness with a grin. Then he entered the room.

She motioned to a wide bench near the wall.

"Please sit down," she said warmly, making him feel at home. "Just a moment. I'll make some coffee." She disappeared in the kitchen.

DeKok sat down and looked around. The room was tastefully furnished. Old, new, antique, modern, balanced in a near perfect harmony. A cast-iron, spiral stairway with teak threads had been cunningly made part of the interior. The room could not be imagined in any other way.

There was a picture of a girl in nurse's uniform on a small, Swedish desk in one corner of the room. The desk was shaded by an unlit floor lamp. DeKok could not see who it was.

Kristel returned from the kitchen with a set of transparent, glass balls and a complicated looking contraption. Somewhere near the bottom a flame caused the coffee to percolate through the system. The smell was heavenly. With an elegant leg she pushed a small table closer, placed the contraption on it and added cups and other ingredients.

"Cream and sugar?"

DeKok nodded.

She sat down next to him and poured.

"I'm glad you came," she said softly. "It was quite a relief. You see, all day I've been dreading this hour, this time. Nanette and I always drink coffee, together, at this time. It was a sort of ritual: close the shop, make coffee."

"I understand completely," nodded DeKok.

She stirred her cup.

"We only had each other. We were dependent on each other."

DeKok looked at her from the side.

49

"You didn't have visitors?"

"We have no girl-friends."

"What about male visitors?"

A blush appeared on her cheeks.

"I have always, categorically, discouraged male visitors."

"Why?"

She sighed.

"We were just two girls together and I didn't want any loose talk."

"This is Amsterdam, not Aalsmeer," grinned DeKok.

"You think it makes a difference?" She looked at him sharply.

DeKok did not answer. Then he asked:

"What did Nanette think about that?"

She took a hasty swallow of her coffee.

"Nanette, Nanette accepted it."

"So, she didn't agree?"

Her face became hard.

"She accepted it."

DeKok sighed.

"I wonder," he thought aloud, "what Nanette's reaction would be if she were to suddenly come in and see us together?"

Kristel turned her face toward the door. Her eyes were large and scared. "No! Nanette? No, that's impossible," she said.

She grabbed DeKok's arm.

"No, no," she almost screamed. "No, that's impossible. That shouldn't be." There was terror in her voice. "Mr. DeKok, please, tell me it's impossible for her to just come in like that, unexpected!?"

DeKok shook his head.

"Don't worry," he said calmly, "with two bolts on the front door that would be quite a trick."

His sarcasm escaped her.

"I'm afraid, Mr. DeKok."

He looked at her searchingly, trying to penetrate to the thoughts beyond the enchanting exterior.

"Of what? Of whom? Nanette? She's dead, isn't she?"

"Yes, yes, she's dead," she panted. Her breasts moved convulsively.

DeKok rubbed his face with his hand. He had come full circle. He was as far as this morning, after Vledder's heavy handed attack. But DeKok was not looking for a fight. He was looking for a calm interview with time and opportunity for confidences. He doubted that he would succeed, however. There was something wrong with Kristel van Daalen. Something he did not understand. He kept missing it. She seemed so, so ... schizoid, so unstable. Sometimes she would appear infinitely desirable and enchanting. But then, suddenly, without warning, she would change into a harpy, react strongly, rebellious, as if she felt threatened. Was Nanette's disappearance the only reason for the mood changes?

He looked at the beautiful woman next to him. So close, he thought, and yet so far away. He looked at the pale face. She was still overwrought. Calmly he drank his coffee and waited until she would calm down herself.

"Could I see her room now?"

She rose and pointed at the spiral staircase.

"Just go upstairs and push the trap door at the top of the stairs, it's counter balanced."

DeKok nodded. He did not yet know how he would identify Nanette's room. It was actually no more than an impulse. He wanted to know what the room looked like. That was all. The color of the curtains, the fabric of her night clothes. DeKok felt that these things were important. They helped him to form a mental picture of the girl he was looking for.

Upstairs Kristel showed him around.

In the back there was an additional work room, or atelier. Red earthenware flower pots were spread all over the floor and the walls were covered with racks and shelves, loaded with beads, various kinds of glasswork, straw and raffia in various lengths and sizes in a riot of colors. There were spools of green wire and plastic ribbons in different colors and widths. It smelled of earth and rotting moss.

Nanette's room was a disappointment. It was a functional bedroom, without frills. Sparsely furnished. A single bed, without cover, was set along one wall, next to a small make-up table. There seemed to be an large collection of make-up articles, almost schematically arranged. A large chest stood against the opposite wall. DeKok opened the doors. To the left was an extensive collection of coats, suits and dresses. To the right, on shelves, were sweaters, shirts and a stack of panties. The top one was green. DeKok read the word *Thursday*, in embroidered letters. He lifted it up and discovered a pink pair of panties with *Friday*, a sky blue set with *Saturday* and yellow panties with *Sunday*.

Monday, Tuesday and Wednesday were missing.

Softly DeKok closed the large chest doors. He looked around one more time and left the room. He had seen enough. Letters, personal papers, or a diary were not present.

Kristel lead the way along the corridor. Along the way she stopped in front of another door.

"And this is my room," she said.

DeKok looked at her. Her face had regained the warm expression of happy generosity. Her blue eyes mirrored a sea of promises.

"Would you like to see it?"

"Please."

Suddenly shy, she slowly opened the door, as if reluctant to reveal a part of herself, to reveal a secret. There was a comfortable aura of feminine intimacy about the room. It reminded one of the closeness of a boudoir of a previous century. But, almost in shrill contrast, a photo in a modern frame was placed on the night table. It showed an athletic girl in shorts, carrying a tennis racket. She noticed DeKok's glance and smiled.

"That's past history. I almost never play anymore."

"Why not?"

"No time. The business takes all my spare time."

DeKok nodded.

"Did Nanette practice any sports?" he asked. "Did she have any hobbies?"

She shook her head.

"Nanette, no, Nanette was just beautiful."

DeKok looked at her searchingly. There was something in her voice that he did not like.

"Have you," he began, hesitating, "have you . . . eh, ever been in love?"

Annoyed, she looked at him.

"In love?"

"Yes, in love. It's normal for girls, young women, young people in general."

He noticed the blue in her eyes change to a steely gray. Her eyes flashed.

"What has that got to do with Nanette's disappearance?"

DeKok made a tired gesture.
"That's exactly what I'm wondering about."

5

DeKok held a lonely vigil behind his desk in the deserted detective room. It was hot. The temperature seemed to resemble that inside a kiln. If it did not, it certainly was not for lack of trying. DeKok had lit one of the giant gas radiators near the window. Nearby, on a hanger, he had draped his raincoat. The coat waved in the hot, shimmering air. He was determined to dry it. His hat, too. He had promised himself dry clothes and, by george, he was going to have dry clothes. He was determined not to leave the room until his immediate goals had been achieved. Even if he was informed, at this very moment, that half the city had been murdered, dry clothes had to come first, then a long time nothing and then, only then, everything else. The annoyed look on his face was emphasized by the stubborn set of his jaws.

DeKok was not in a good humor. The interview with Kristel van Daalen had not gone according to plan. He would have liked to see some more forthrightness, a little more trust. But she kept evading him. As long as he remained under the influence of her physical beauty, as long as he seemed spell-bound thereby, she would be all sweetness and light. But no sooner did he struggle away from her captivating spell, tried to become the city official, asking questions, needing to know the answers to facts, no sooner did he try to do his job, in other words, and she would become furious. She would actually snort. It was a strange situation, he thought, cousin Kristel asks help from the police regarding the disappearance of cousin Nanette. But as soon as the police started to ask questions, the self-same Kristel clammed up like an oyster. He could not resist smiling at the mixed metaphor.

He loosened the top button of his shirt and looked thoughtfully at the heat, shimmering above the radiator. I should just withdraw from the case, he thought. Just issue an APB and let the consequences be the consequences, let the chips fall where they may, so to speak. If the interested parties were not going to cooperate, why should he worry his head about it? After all, it was probably quite understandable why Nanette had taken off. *I have always, categorically, discouraged male visitors.* He grinned to himself. His grin remained his most attractive feature. Did Kristel really expect to keep love outside by that attitude? Why? It was rather silly. He took a blank Text Form and thought about what he wanted to write. After some deliberation, he decided on an blanket APB, including the border posts.

He wrote:

The Commissaris of Police, Chief 2nd Division, Post Warmoes Street in Amsterdam, requests to be informed of the whereabouts of Nanette Bogaard, age nineteen. Description: Approximately 5 foot 6 inches; slender; long, blond hair with natural wave. Last seen dressed in dark-blue suit of skirt and jacket and . . .

He put the pen down.

Suddenly he remembered what he had seen in Nanette's room. The panties with the days of the week. He pressed his lips together and shook his head. Something was wrong, something did not add up. According to Kristel, Nanette had disappeared yesterday, on Thursday. But the panties with *Thursday* were still in the closet. If Nanette really was in the habit—and it seemed that way—if she really was in the habit of changing her panties everyday, according to the day written on it, then Kristel had been lying. Then, Nanette had not disappeared on Thursday, but was already gone on Wednesday.

Suddenly DeKok began to laugh. All by himself and loudly. It was high time that he took a long, sober look at Nanette's case. He was getting upset over nothing, started to see suspects in every corner. Never mind the panties. That was ridiculous, of course it was. After all, what woman was going to be dictated by the days written on a pair of panties? One in a thousand? Perhaps! Probably less than that. In his mind's eye he could visualize himself in front of the Judge: "And then, Your Honor, I saw in the closet those panties ... eh, ladies' garments . . ., underwear, Your Honor, and . . . eh, embroidered thereupon . . ." The defense would have a field day with it. The telephone on his desk started to ring. He lifted the receiver. It was Vledder.

"I'm back from Aalsmeer."

"All right. Where are you now?"

"At the station house near the Stadium. I just called to see if you were still there."

"Why?"

"Well, if you had gone home, then I would have gone home as well. I have a date tonight, you see, with a girl."

"So?"

"Yes. Yes, well, but if you had planned anything for tonight, you see."

"Have you known her for some time?"

57

"Who?"

"The girl."

"About three months."

DeKok thought for a while.

"Does she wear panties with the days on it?"

"What!?"

"You know, panties, with days embroidered on it. One for every day."

He heard Vledder sputter.

"It's never gone that . . . eh, I mean, . . . eh, it's rather an intimate piece of apparel."

"Right, that's what this is all about. It was just a shot in the dark. Apparently the sexual revolution of today's youth is less a reality than seems apparent. You just keep your date."

There was silence on the line for a while.

"DeKok, are you going to be in the office much longer?"

"Oh, maybe another half hour, or so."

"OK, then I'll see you shortly."

"Why, have you discovered anything important, in Aalsmeer?"

"No, but you talk funny."

It sounded worried.

"Go to hell!"

DeKok threw the receiver down and used his handkerchief to wipe the sweat off his forehead. It was getting hotter in the room. He was just about ready to shut the radiator off, when the phone rang again. This time it was the desk sergeant, downstairs.

"Somebody down here, who's asking for Inspector DeKok, with kay-oh-kay."

"What kind of somebody?"

"A young man, about twenty-seven with . . ."

"... dark-blond hair and dark glasses," completed DeKok.

"Precisely."

"Is he alone?"

"Yes."

"Fine, just send him up, will you?"

DeKok replaced the receiver and hastened to turn the radiator off. He was starting to melt. His hands stuck to every surface he touched.

He took his coat from the hanger and opened the window for some fresh air. It had finally stopped raining, he noticed. From his vantage point he looked down on small groups of people in the street. It was busy in the streets. A lot of noise was generated by the bars across the street from the station. A lonely man, unseen, sang a sad song. *'Mother, I cannot live without you . . .'* understood DeKok. It sounded convincing. A real tear-jerker. There was a knock on the door.

DeKok closed the window and walked back to his desk. Meanwhile he took his jacket off. He was still sweating. With the sleeve of his shirt he dried his face. He draped his jacket over the back of his chair and rolled his shirt sleeves up. Only then did he call:

"Enter!"

The door opened slowly and the young man, whom he had first met in Little Lowee's bar, entered with obvious reluctance.

DeKok smiled encouragingly and pointed at the chair next to his desk.

"Sit down, my friend," he said in a friendly tone of voice.

The young man showed antagonism in his face.

"I'm not your friend."

DeKok grimaced.

"You're right," he admitted in a resigned sort of voice. "As far as that's concerned, one cannot be selective enough. But, . . . eh, what can I do for you?"

The young man swallowed.

"What's the matter with Nanette?"

DeKok moved his eyebrows. Those who knew him well, swore that DeKok's eyebrows sometimes showed a life of their own. They could actually ripple. Vledder could stare at them for minutes at a time, mesmerized.

"I thought you weren't interested?" asked DeKok finally.

"I'm sorry, but I am, interested, I mean."

DeKok sighed.

"But this afternoon . . .," he began,

"That was this afternoon," interrupted the young man, irritated. "I could hardly admit I was interested in front of the lady I was with. I mean, how would I explain to her that I was interested in the disappearance of a girl, a specific girl, even."

"But why not? Pearl isn't jealous."

"Pearl?" the young man asked, surprised. "You know her?"

DeKok smiled.

"Black Pearl of Cuba, oh yes. Sometimes, when she's in a good mood, she'll call herself the Jamaican Whirlwind, or the Caribbean Hurricane." He snorted depreciatingly. "Not that it means a whole lot, but for a virtually unknown singer in small bars, it always sounds so much better than Black Mary from Rotterdam."

The young man stroked his lips with his hands.

"You . . . eh, you're well informed."

DeKok shrugged his shoulders.

"Ach," he said, almost apologetically, "that doesn't mean a lot in the case of Pearl. Almost every guy in the neighborhood could have told you the same. It's really an open secret. I think, Mr. Bogaard, that she's interested in you, because you're relatively new to the neighborhood."

"What do you mean by new?"

Smiling, DeKok leaned closer.

"What are you hoping to find in the neighborhood, Mr. Bogaard?"

"Nothing, I live here, near the Old Seadike."

"What are you hoping to find, I asked?"

"I . . . eh, I told you, I live here."

DeKok leaned even closer. His face almost touched the face of the young man next to his desk. He whispered.

"Mr. Bogaard, how long have you been sick?"

The young man started to laugh nervously.

"Sick . . . I . . . sick?"

DeKok nodded emphatically.

"Yes, you, how long?"

The young man became more and more restless. More anxious. DeKok did not miss any of it. The eyes moved restlessly behind the dark glasses. The hands, although pressed flat against the knees, shook.

"How long?" repeated DeKok in a compelling voice.

Bogaard did not answer.

Then, suddenly, after a few flashing movements, DeKok held him in a grip like steel. Holding the young man's wrist with one hand, he pushed a sleeve up with the other hand. It happened so fast, was so totally unexpected, that even if the man had expected it, he could not have prevented it. Accusingly, incontrovertibly, the pale, naked inner arm of Bogaard was exposed in DeKok's grip. The tracks and puncture marks spoke their own, clear language.

"Morphine?"

The young man nodded silently. His handsome face had a sad, almost painful expression. His lower lip quivered, as with a child, ready to burst into tears.

DeKok let go of the arm and felt pity.

"If I hurt you," he said, concerned, "I'm sorry. Such was not my intent. But I had to know what bothered you. You understand, you're not the type one finds in this neighborhood. Therefore, I wondered ..."

Bogaard pulled his sleeve down and adjusted his clothes.

"Happy now?" It sounded bitter.

DeKok looked at him, suspiciously.

"Why should I be happy? Because you're sick? Addicted to morphine? I should be happy about that? What do you take me for, Mr. Bogaard? A sadist? Somebody who enjoys your misery?"

"Perhaps."

DeKok did not react at once. He looked at the young man for some time, silent, a thoughtful expression on his face.

"You're right," he said after a while. "Perhaps, but it will always be perhaps. You cannot read my mind and I cannot read yours. And we're all guilty of mouthing one sentiment, at times, while thinking the exact opposite." He made a wry gesture with his hands. "The cause of many a misunderstanding," he concluded.

At that moment Vledder entered the detective room in his usual, exuberant way. He hung his coat on a peg and looked surprised from DeKok to the young man and back again.

"You still have visitors?"

DeKok smiled.

"Let me introduce you to Mr. Bogaard."

Vledder tried to ripple his eyebrows, but as usual, had to settle for wrinkling his forehead.

"Bogaard?" he asked.

The young man rose and shook hands with Vledder.

"My mother's name. I . . . eh, I write under that name."

"You write?" asked DeKok.

A bitter smile played around the lips of the young man.

"Never heard of Frank Bogaard?"

Vledder's eyes glistened. He nodded emphatically.

"Of course, of course. I've read your books. *The Quiet End* and *The Transparent Death*. Both books caused rather a sensation, some years back. It was a rather somber future you predicted in your books, if I remember correctly. In any case, I devoured both books. Especially among young adults your books had quite an impact, as I remember it, right?"

Bogaard sighed.

"Yes, especially among young adults. Most of the older generation have rejected my books. They were found to be too negative, too nihilistic." He grinned. "As if an A-Bomb is something to cheer about."

DeKok sat down again. He had never read anything by Frank Bogaard, but he could imagine the trend of his books. Life without hope. Death without release. It did not seem attractive reading material.

"Bogaard, you said, is your mother's name?"

"Yes."

"So Nanette isn't your sister?"

"No, Nanette is my cousin."

"Exactly. And when did you see her last?"

The young man pulled on his lower lip.

"About two weeks ago, I think."

"Where?"

"In my room, here in the Quarter. She came to visit me. After my mother's death, Nanette was the only one in my family who still had anything to do with me."

"Why? Are you a black sheep?"

Frank smiled.

"You could say that. My way of life, I think. My thoughts, ideas. They're not exactly in line with what is expected of somebody with a middle class background. And the Van Daalen family is very middle class."

DeKok looked at him, his head cocked.

"Van Daalen with double a?"

"Yes, my father is Martin van Daalen, a grower."

"And Kristel?"

"Kristel is my sister."

DeKok raked his hands through his hair. He had to absorb this information slowly. His glance fell on the face of the young man. There were some similarities, minute similarities. Frank van Daalen's face was more delineated, sharper. The signs of his addiction were easy to read. The addiction had deepened the creases in his face, affected the skin tone.

"Did she ever visit you?"

"Who? Kristel?"

"Yes."

The young man grinned without mirth.

"I don't think she even knows where I live. She certainly doesn't know I live in Amsterdam. You see, we've become more and more estranged over the last few years." Reflecting, he looked past DeKok, apparently overcome by memories. Then he continued: "It used to be so different, before, when we were younger, yes, then, we really liked each other."

"No longer?"

Sadly he shook his head.

"Kristel," he said slowly, "Kristel, has remained a Van Daalen."

DeKok nodded his understanding.

"And you became a Bogaard?"

Frank lifted his glasses and rubbed his eyes with a tired gesture.

"Yes, I became a Bogaard."

They remained silent. After a while DeKok rose and walked to the small counter and the percolator. He felt like a cup of coffee. He filled the pot from the tap, put coffee in the top of the percolator and placed the assembled unit on the flame. DeKok liked the old-fashioned percolator. He did not believe in the modern, electric coffee makers.

Vledder pushed his chair closer to young Bogaard.

"When," he asked, genuinely interested, "will you publish your next book?"

The face of the young man became even more somber.

"That, . . . eh, that I don't know. That's . . . eh, difficult to say. You never know, exactly, when inspiration will hit you. Sometimes it stays away for a long, long time. Sometimes it's gone forever."

DeKok with his back to the two men, seemed to detect a tone of anxiety, of fear. Slowly he turned toward them.

"What was your last book, Bogaard?"

The young man hesitated momentarily.

"*The Transparent Death*," he said with a sigh.

Vledder looked shocked.

"*The Transparent Death*?" he asked, "but . . . eh, that's quiet some time ago, isn't it?"

"Yes, four years." it sounded dispirited. "I wrote *The Transparent Death* four years ago. It took less than three months to write. Completely. I wrote almost every day and

65

every night. As one possessed. When I turned the manuscript in to the publisher I had a feeling of immense release, as if I had been freed from a demon, something compelling. But the publisher merely said: 'Give me another one'."

He took off his dark glasses and hid his face in his hands.

"It became a torture, it haunted me. Suddenly I had lost it. I was finished, written out. Writer's block. Ha! Writer's disability was more like it. No matter what I tried, it was impossible. My head seemed to me a vast, hollow space. Nothing, absolutely nothing. No thoughts left. No feelings, no content. I was empty, drained, completely drained."

Suddenly he started to sob like a child. His body shook. He lifted his head. His large, wet eyes looked beseechingly at DeKok. His lips quivered and his hands stretched toward the gray sleuth.

"Where is Nanette?" he cried.

DeKok did not answer. Searchingly he looked at the young man. Without the dark glasses the similarity between him and Kristel was much more noticeable, especially the shape and color of the eyes.

"Where is Nanette?"

The young man's voice was close to hysteria.

"Where is Nanette?" he screamed.

DeKok remained outwardly unmoved. His sharp eyes registered every nuance, every movement. He noticed how the body started to shake almost convulsively. The mouth pulled in nervous tics. It was frightening, terrifying. The face lost all color, it became white as marble. Cold sweat appeared on the skin.

"Nanette!" it sounded like a death's knell.

Completely agitated, he got out of the chair and started to wave his arms around. His movements resembled those of a man, being pulled down into a maelstrom, trying to reach a life belt, just out of reach.

Vledder took hold of Bogaard from behind, around the waist; spoke to him, forceful, convincingly, calming. Nothing helped. The young man continued to scream, out of his mind, foam on the lips.

"Na-nette!!"

DeKok looked on from his place next to the percolator. He did not interfere. He knew it was useless, it would not take much longer.

Bogaard swayed suddenly; a grotesque movement, without sense, or volition. Then his muscles relaxed. His eyes glassed over. The head fell sideways. A deep sigh escaped from his chest. Slowly the body slid from Vledder's arms onto the floor.

6

The impassive paramedics did not say much. They placed the weak, exhausted body of Frank Bogaard on the stretcher, arranged a blanket over him and tightened the broad leather straps. Then they carefully lifted the stretcher and carried it down the long corridor. Almost vertically, they maneuvered it down the tight staircase to the ground floor. It went simply, easy, routinely. It was a quiet demonstration of compassion and great experience.

DeKok walked down the stairs, behind the stretcher.

The desk sergeant made a vague gesture toward the stretcher and raised his eyebrows.

"Hey, DeKok," he grinned, "what do I put in my report? Another victim of the Third Degree?"

DeKok did not appreciate the coarse humor.

"Just report: Man sick, probably because of slow poisoning as a result of abuse of a controlled substance," he answered mildly.

The desk sergeant snorted.

"He must be ready for his next fix, more likely," he remarked. He looked at the pale face on the stretcher and pushed his lower lip forward. "They say you should pity them. I suppose so." It did not sound very convincing. "How did he get here, anyway?"

"He reported to you, a while ago, don't you remember? You sent him upstairs yourself," answered DeKok.

The desk sergeant thought. A pained expression showed on his face.

"You're right," he admitted, "the pale one, with the dark glasses. I rang you." He took a note pad and dictated to himself: "Man appeared under own volition, at this station and left, via ambulance to . . ."

He looked at the paramedics.

"Where are you taking him?"

They put the stretcher down.

"To 'Old Willy'," answered the older one.

". . . Wilhelmina Hospital," wrote the sergeant.

"What do you think?" asked DeKok. "Are they going to keep him in the hospital, or are they going to let him go as soon as he recovers?"

The older paramedic shook his head.

"They're going to keep him in observation, at least for a few days. If it's really bad, they'll keep him and put him in for withdrawal. That's the usual procedure, anyway."

"And then?"

"Just hope they don't start again. Because if they get hold of even the smallest dose, they're hooked again."

The second paramedic nodded agreement.

They picked up the stretcher once more and walked out of the station. The ambulance was backed up to the front door. A constable helped them load.

* * *

The smell of coffee greeted DeKok when he returned to the detective room. Vledder had finished making the coffee and prepared two mugs.

"Gone?"

DeKok sat down behind his desk. With both hands around the mug he began to slurp his coffee. A most unattractive sound. His thoughts were with Frank Bogaard, his dependency on drugs and his wild desire for his cousin. The cry of 'Na-nette' still sounded in his ears. Resonated within his brain.

"Is he gone?" repeated Vledder.

DeKok nodded.

"For the time being, they're taking him to the Wilhelmina Hospital, for observation. Perhaps they'll put him in for drug rehab, that is, if he plans to cooperate. It's, of course, the only cure."

Vledder sighed, then he said:

"Can you fathom it? Such a talented, intelligent guy. You'd expect that such a man would know what the inevitable results would be. If you persist, you go to hell, everybody knows that."

DeKok replaced his mug on the desk.

"If you persist . . . ," he repeated slowly.

"What do you mean?"

"No more than what I said. If you persist. You see, nobody plans to become enslaved. Nobody believes they can get hooked. Everybody thinks that they are the exception, they can quit whenever they want to. One starts, a small dose at first, just a remedy, really. Perhaps to help you over a temporary difficulty, a pain, a physical thing, or maybe a mental thing. For instance, writer's block."

Vledder looked surprised.

"You seriously believe that's why Bogaard started to take drugs?"

DeKok shrugged his shoulders.

"I don't know. I really don't know. Perhaps. We really don't know enough about our friend to come to any definitive conclusions. In any case, he's been hooked for some time. Judging by his physical deterioration, I would guess at least a year. Perhaps longer. The best thing is to check with the doctor, tomorrow. Meanwhile we have a very important question to answer."

"Question?"

DeKok nodded.

"Yes, how did Frank Bogaard get the stuff. Who was his supplier?"

Carelessly Vledder shrugged his shoulders.

"Considering the area in which he lives, near the Old Seadike, practically in the heart of the Quarter, that seems to be less of a problem. There are plenty of contacts. Personally I think that he moved into the Quarter in order to be closer to his source of supply. Otherwise, what could he possibly be looking for, there."

DeKok did not answer at once. He had a very annoying habit of ignoring things, when he wanted to do so. But this time that was not the case. With the hands under his chin, both elbows firmly on the edge of the desk, he looked thoughtfully at nothing in particular. A sudden thought occupied his mind.

"You know," he said suddenly, "addiction can cause people to do the strangest things. Even the meekest may be moved to violent acts. When they can't satisfy their need, when they're unable to get their fix, when their drug is withheld, they're liable to do anything. Even murder."

Amazed Vledder looked at DeKok.

"You're not thinking that Frank Bo . . .," he did not finish the sentence.

"What?"

"You're not thinking that Frank Bogaard has anything to do with Nanette's disappearance?"

"What's so strange about that?"

"Nothing, no, but . . ."

DeKok stood up from his chair and started to pace across the dusty floor of the detective room. His thoughts were more easily arranged to the beat of his shuffling gait.

"What did Frank Bogaard do?" he asked in the tone of a professor in front of a class, "what did he do when he became uncomfortable, just now?"

Almost mechanically, Vledder answered:

"He went into convulsions and started to cry out."

"Exactly, he started to cry out. For what?"

"For whom, rather. For Nanette."

"Why?"

Vledder shrugged his shoulders.

"He wanted her, . . . eh, he needed her?"

"What for?"

"I don't know."

DeKok halted in front of Vledder.

"All right, taking into account his addiction, what did Frank need more than anything, at that time?"

"His next fix."

DeKok nodded approvingly.

"Exactly! And what did he call for?"

"Nanette!"

Suddenly there was a gleam in young Vledder's eyes.

"Of course," he exclaimed, "he called Nanette, but he meant morphine!"

DeKok raised an index finger in a most pedantic manner.

"And what does that mean?" he asked.

"That means," answered Vledder, suddenly very serious, "that in Franks's mind the concepts morphine and Nanette are closely interrelated. There is really almost no difference."

DeKok let himself down in his chair.

"In other words, Nanette was his supplier."

Sighing, Vledder shook his head.

"My stars," he said, still shocked by the quick succession of startling thoughts, "Nanette Bogaard, the wild daisy from *Ye Three Roses*, is also a drug dealer."

"Whoa, there, my young friend, don't go overboard there. She supplied Frank, perhaps, although I'm almost certain. But if she was indeed a dealer, a pusher, in the sense that you describe, that we don't know. At the very least it is a premature suspicion."

Vledder grinned.

"Premature? First of all, we can safely assume that Frank paid dearly for his pleasures. We're not going to assume, I hope, that Nanette delivered free of charge?"

DeKok pulled on his lower lip and let it plop back. He repeated the gesture. A most annoying sound.

"Free of charge? No, street prices are pretty hefty. But I don't think that Nanette was in it for the money. You remember what Kristel told us: Nanette wasn't interested in money, she couldn't care less."

"Yes, yes," exclaimed Vledder, animated, "that's what Kristel said. But how far can we trust her? Perhaps that entire flower shop, *Ye Three Roses*, is no more than a front for an extensive traffic in drugs."

DeKok laughed heartily.

74

"Oh, yes, for sure," he mocked, "I can see it now, a field full of poppies at the ancestral home site, in Aalsmeer, and an opium distillery borrowed from *The Three Bottles*, down the street."

Vledder pulled a face, discouraged by DeKok's cynical tone.

"Well, yes, if you put it that way," he said, almost shyly, "it was only a theory, you know."

DeKok grinned. It remained his most attractive feature. The old, experienced, craggy face would become almost boyish.

"Well, don't let it get you down. I was only joking. You're right. The flower shop could be an ideal front. But I don't believe it. No, I don't believe it at all, at all. It requires a completely different set-up and different characters, more cunning, more calculating, more callous. I went to *Ye Three Roses* this afternoon. I had Kristel show me around. I talked to her . . ." He smiled softly to himself. "It was a bit exciting, at times. Kristel van Daalen is an extremely beautiful woman, you know. Especially within her own environment, her own sphere of influence." Dreamily he stared in the distance, as if fascinated by his own thoughts.

Vledder looked searchingly at his old mentor.

"And?" he asked.

Absent mindedly DeKok looked up.

"Oh, nothing, no. I mean, well, . . . eh, I didn't get any farther. That's to say, I don't know any more then we knew this morning."

It was Vledder's turn to grin.

". . . Nanette Bogaard has disappeared and beautiful Kristel expects the worst. That's the way it is . . . isn't it?"

"Yes. Yes, my boy, that's the way it is."

At that moment the phone rang.

Vledder lifted the receiver.

"Am I speaking to Inspector DeKok?"

"No, just a moment."

He passed the receiver to DeKok.

"It's for you."

DeKok pulled his chair closer to the desk.

"This is DeKok, who's calling?"

"Never mind that," said the voice at the other end of the line, "I just want to help you in the right direction, is all."

"What direction . . . with what?"

"You'll find out, Mr. DeKok. I advise you to take a look on the Mirror's Canal."

"The Mirror's Canal?"

"Yes, the quiet side of the water."

"And what will I find there?"

The line remained silent for a while. A pause. Someone was obviously deliberating.

"Are you interested in antiques?"

"Not especially."

"Well, then it's about time you start paying some attention to it. Believe me, it'll be worth your while. Good night, Mr. DeKok."

"Good night, . . . eh, . . ."

The connection was broken.

For several seconds DeKok remained motionless, the receiver still in his hand, clamped to one ear. He was searching among the confusing relics in the attic of his brain . . . a memory . . . a point of reference. He did not find anything that gave him a clue. He could not place the voice. The insistent buzzing of an occupied line broke his concentration. Softly he replaced the receiver.

"Who was it?" asked Vledder.

DeKok shrugged his shoulders.

76

"An unknown lover of antiques, I think. I was advised to take a look on the quiet side of the Mirror's Canal."

"For what?"

"Antiques, I think. You'll find that both sides of the Mirror's Canal are occupied by antiques stores, or stores that purport to be antique stores. Almost shoulder to shoulder." He stood up and shuffled over to the hat-stand, grabbing for his raincoat and his decrepit little hat.

"I think we should take a look," he said.

"Now, at once?" Vledder voiced his surprise.

"Why not?"

Vledder sighed.

"What if it's a joke?"

DeKok made a helpless gesture.

"Well, then at least somebody will be amused."

7

DeKok drove through the old inner city of Amsterdam. Nimbly, bold like a taxi driver, he managed to squeeze the old VW through the various traffic obstacles, other traffic and the thousands upon thousands of bicycles. He was enjoying himself. A happy smile played around his lips. He loved the unknown. It attracted him, irresistibly. That was the main reason for reacting so immediately and so spontaneously to the strange tip over the telephone. Ridiculous, if one stopped to think about it, almost like some boyish adventure. He wondered what he would find on the Mirror's Canal. What did the mysterious caller want him to find? Would it really show a connection with the disappearance of Nanette?

Past the Town Hall, he turned along the Emperor's Canal, waited patiently for the red light at the corner of Leiden Street and parked, shortly thereafter, at the intersection of the New Mirror Street and the Mirror's Canal. He dimmed the lights and turned the ignition off.

Vledder sprawled in the seat next to him. The knees pressed against the dashboard. His young face bore a glum look. He showed no desire to get out of the car. DeKok looked at him from the side.

"We're here, my boy," he said, friendly and encouraging. "Would you rather have gone on your date, after all?"

Vledder pushed himself into a sitting position.

"It isn't that. You know that. If necessary, I'm ready to go night and day with you, step by step and hour after hour, even if you wanted to go to the North Pole."

DeKok grinned expansively.

"Such loyalty!"

Abruptly, Vledder turned toward him.

"Loyal, yes, loyal, that's me. But also forthright. You see, I don't use dirty police tricks on my colleagues."

DeKok looked at him in amazement.

"Dirty police tricks?"

"Yes, dirty police tricks. If you had to know so urgently, I mean, if you really wanted to know how it is, between me and my girl, you could have just asked me. It wasn't necessary to use any of your transparent interrogation tricks on me." He imitated DeKok's voice with devastating effectiveness: "Does she wear panties with the days on it?" He snorted. "What do you care what sort of panties Celine wears?"

With difficulty DeKok managed to suppress a loud, boisterous laugh. It caused a slight pain in his chest.

"Oh, oh," he said, finally, "so her name's Celine?"

"Yes," answered Vledder sharply, "and she isn't at all the sort of girl that you apparently envision."

DeKok turned in his seat and put a reassuring hand on Vledder's shoulder.

"Listen, my boy," he said convincingly, in a fatherly tone of voice, "I really wasn't trying to satisfy any morbid curiosity and I most certainly was not trying to practice any 'dirty police tricks' on you. Please take my word for that. I'll explain later, in more detail. As far as Celine is concerned,

I'm sure she's a very dear girl. You most certainly seem to have fallen for her, and not just a little, either. I wouldn't mind meeting her."

Vledder looked at him suspiciously.

"You mean that?"

"Yes, you should introduce her," nodded DeKok. "As soon as possible. How about next Sunday? I'll tell my wife to organize a little party. Why not?"

Vledder's expression changed. It became happier and sunnier. He was obviously mollified.

"Yes, that sounds like a great idea," he said with sudden enthusiasm. "Yes, we'll do that. We'll come. You can count on that. Yes, we'll look forward to it."

Vledder's moods had a habit of changing rather quickly, at times.

DeKok looked at him once more, the eyebrows started to vibrate, as if in preparation of their famous dance across his forehead.

"From where I sit," he said slowly, "this may well be the love of your life. Yes, Love with a Capital L." He nodded to himself.

"What do you mean?"

"You're already speaking in *pluralis majestatis*."

"In what!?"

DeKok grinned.

"*Pluralis majestatis*," he lectured, "plural as in 'royal' plural. You know, as in 'We, Edward, by the grace of God, King . . .' The press uses the same sort of plural form. And old, married couples, of course. It's a disease. We this and we that. After a few years of marriage it has been known to be incurable."

* * *

There was nobody in sight on the Mirror's Canal. Nobody. The roadway on both sides of the Canal was completely deserted. On one side a car would pass occasionally. Blinking turn signals as it rounded the corner. On the quiet side of the Canal nothing stirred at all.

Vledder and DeKok had divided the task. Alert and prepared for anything, they both started at one end of the Canal and approached each other. But nothing in particular attracted their attention. They met in the middle.

Vledder shrugged his shoulders.

"Nothing, absolutely nothing. I think somebody pulled a joke on us." He gestured at the dark houses around. "Perhaps they're watching us even now, from behind a darkened window. Laughing. Who knows."

DeKok pushed his hat farther back on his head.

"I don't believe it's a joke," he said seriously. "We've only just looked around a bit, skimmed the surface, so to speak. We were told to pay attention to antiques. We haven't done that yet."

"What do you want?" asked Vledder. "Do you really want to look in the store fronts of all these shops?"

"There seems no other way," nodded DeKok.

Vledder started to grin to himself.

"What are we looking for? Oil-fired lamps, nightstands with artistic worm holes? Bed warmers, silver candlesticks, rusty weather vanes, chamber pots. Tell me, what's your preference?"

DeKok looked at his pupil with a slightly disapproving look.

"Just think," he said patiently. "If this is a real tip, not a wild goose chase, then the tipster wants us to find something, has a reason. He wants us to discover something, wants us to see it."

"Understandable, but what?" Vledder grimaced.

"Simple. Something that we would not recognize at first glance, but of which the tipster expects us to draw conclusions. You understand, it must be a recognizable hint, no matter what direction it leads. We're looking for the hint, not necessarily the object. Otherwise the phone call would make no sense at all. You see?"

"Well, it's clear as mud, but it covers the ground," nodded Vledder. Sometimes he could mix metaphors with the best of them.

"All right, then. You start from the side of the Prince's Canal and I start from the other side. Look carefully. Look at everything you see and try to visualize if any of the items could contain a hint we can use. If you find something that, no matter how strange, draws your attention, you call me."

"Ok, boss."

They separated and started each on their own end of the short Canal. Slowly they ambled from one store to the next. A wild kaleidoscope of old objects passed by them, displayed helter-skelter in a number of dusty, little shops, small store fronts and even some basement windows. Again they met approximately in the middle.

"And?"

Sadly Vledder shook his head.

"I saw nothing in particular. And you?"

DeKok rubbed his hands over his face.

"No," he admitted soberly, "me neither. Scales, statues, unmatched chairs, flower pots, lanterns, frames, more statues. The same junk everywhere."

Vledder laughed.

"Come," he said, cajolingly, "let's go home."

He took the gray sleuth by the arm and tried to pull him toward the car.

"Tomorrow is another day. It's been enough for today."
He looked at his watch. "It's almost midnight."

DeKok could not be moved. He stood his ground, stubborn. He scratched underneath his hat.

"There's got to be something," he exclaimed irritated. "There must. That call was not for nothing. It had a purpose. Absolutely. I'm old enough to detect the difference between a serious call and a joke. It isn't a joke." He pressed his lips together. "You know what?" he continued vehemently, "we keep looking. I look in the stores you have looked at and you take my half. Understand? There is no other way. We must have missed something."

"OK, boss," answered Vledder, bored.

DeKok looked at him.

"One more *OK, boss*," he said sharply and suddenly full of menace, ". . . and I'll pull a gun on you."

Vledder was shocked by the suddenly changed tone.

"Oh, . . . eh, OK . . ., eh . . ."

DeKok grinned at the reaction.

"All right, my boy," he said, much more friendly all of a sudden. "Let's try it one more time. If we still find nothing, we'll go home."

Again they shuffled from window to window, from one antique store to another. Carefully they looked at the items displayed. Looking for something that might be important enough to move someone to call the police. But who? And why so secretive?

DeKok thought about that. If he only knew who the tipster was, then he would have a better idea what to look for. What sort of item, or clue, was hidden among the junk. While his eyes were scanning the displays, his brains worked on a different level. He was looking for an answer, as well as a clue. But so far, neither his eyes, nor his brains, could come up with a solution. It was like dealing with a computer suffering from an overload of input without a program to organize it.

Lost in thought, he suddenly was startled into awareness of his surroundings. Vledder was standing next to him and tapped him on the shoulder.

"Come on." he said seriously, "I think I found something."

"Where?"

"A couple of doors down."

Meekly, DeKok followed his pupil. Vledder halted in front of an old canal house with a bluestone stoop. He pointed diagonally upward. There was no real store window in the strict sense of the word. Obviously the house had been a residence in the dim past. It had been converted to a store and one of the front windows had become a store window. At least, items were displayed behind the window. The window revealed a room, or what had been a room, now converted to store use. It was dimly lit. All kinds of object were spread out in the shadowy space. DeKok had passed the window twice and had not noticed anything in particular. He looked along the pointing arm of Vledder.

"What are you pointing at?"

"The painting."

"Where?"

"On the wall, just above the antique pistols."

DeKok's glance travelled upward. Suddenly he saw what Vledder meant. It was a large, somewhat dark painting, contained in a broad, heavily gilded frame, decorated with scroll work and arabesques. The canvass had been painted in a simple, figurative style, allowing the contours to softly flow into the background of somber blue and intense purple.

The painting was uncommonly fascinating and DeKok did not understand how he could have missed it before.

It was a nude, seated on a low, old fashioned sofa of red brocade with a backrest edged in a stylized, curving, black wood. The figure of the young woman had been painted with infinite tenderness. The nuances in the soft pink of the skin and the gloss of the long, waving hair bore witness to the intense emotions and loving attention directed at the subject. Although the nude was depicted in realistic detail, there was no hint of either sexual provocation, or stimulating excitement.

On the contrary, the painting reflected an intense calm, a serene, almost exalted modesty.

Utterly fascinated, DeKok was again absorbed by the impressions of color and composition. His glance followed every line of the painting: the long, slender hand, resting on one knee; the sweet swelling of the breasts, the slight arching of the back; the long, gold hair as a separate frame for the fine face, a face that struck him in recognition, but even more so because of the somber look in the eyes.

"Nanette," he whispered softly.

Vledder took a deep breath.

"Yes," he sighed. "Nanette Bogaard. That's what the tipster meant."

For a long time they both stood, speechless. Their noses were almost flattened against the window. The exquisite painting kept them in a near unbreakable spell.

Vledder was first to break the silence.

"I wonder," he said softly, "who could have painted her so somberly?"

DeKok did not answer at once. As if bewitched he stared in the distance. His coarse face was expressionless.

"That's it," he said after a while, "that's it exactly."

Vledder looked at him in surprise.

"What?" he asked.

"The somber nude! The somber nude, I can't think of a better name for the painting."

* * *

DeKok sat down on the bluestone stoop of the antique store. Broadly, immovable, like a human Cerberus with the remarkable face of a good natured boxer.

Vledder stood in front of him and looked down at his mentor. Unable to ripple his eyebrows, he frowned.

"You're surely not planning," he started in a suspicious tone, "to remain on guard her, the rest of the night?"

DeKok rested his head in his hands, elbows on the knees.

"I must have that painting," he said resignedly. "I must have it, no matter how. I must know who painted it."

Slowly he rose, took his notebook from a pocket and wrote down the name and the phone number of the proprietor.

"It's too bad," he sighed, "that the good man doesn't live near, or behind, or even above his shop. Than we could have reached him at once."

He motioned to Vledder.

"Come one," he said, "we're going to call him."

"Now, at this hour?"

"Why not? Antique dealers, so I've been told, always stay up very, very late."

They drove back to the police station, along the deserted streets and canals. As soon as they arrived, DeKok picked up the phone and called the antique dealer. It took a long time before the receiver was picked up at the other end.

"Grevelen here," said a sleepy voice.

"DeKok, Inspector DeKok, with . . . eh, kay-oh-kay. Police, Warmoes Street."

"Homicide?"

"Yes, but don't worry. I just want to let you know that I'm interested in the painting of the somber nude. I saw it in your shop on the Mirror's Canal."

"Interested?"

"Yes, I would appreciate it, if you didn't sell it right-away. You see, I want to take a good look at it, first. I'll be by your shop in the morning."

For a while there was utter silence on the line. Then:

"Say, Mr. DeKok, is there something the matter with that painting?"

"Why?"

"Well, . . . eh, you're already the second person to call me about it."

"The second?"

"Yes, there was a very excited man who wanted to buy the painting, unseen, regardless of price. I thought it rather strange, so over the telephone, you know. I didn't take the call very serious."

"Who was that man? Do you know?"

"Yes I do. Just a moment. I wrote it down, somewhere."

The statement was followed by a few seconds of silence that seemed like an eternity to DeKok. Then the dealer came back on the phone.

"Here it is," he said, "yes, that's who called. One Wielen, a journalist."

8

The next morning when DeKok—late, as had been his habit for many, many years—arrived at the station, Vledder met him halfway across the large detective room.

"Frank Bogaard," he began excitedly, "is gone! Last night he fled from the hospital and the Commissaris wants to see you at once."

DeKok nodded to him in a friendly way.

"Good morning," he called cheerfully, "slept well, did you?"

Vledder swallowed.

"Last night," he tried again, "Frank Bogaard fled ..."

Unperturbed DeKok passed him by.

"Coffee ready?"

"Yes, that's to ... eh, I think so."

"Excellent," warbled DeKok, exuberant. "Excellent, really excellent."

He went to his desk, took his mug from a drawer and poured calmly. Like most older police officers on the force, DeKok lived by the golden Amsterdam rule: The day starts with coffee, or not at all. It was a habit which could simply not be broken. The failure to solve a murder case, in a manner of speaking, was not nearly as serious, as the breaking of *that* tradition of the old, renowned station at the Warmoes Street.

DeKok stirred an exorbitant amount of sugar into his coffee and sat down at his desk. Apart from tradition, he regarded coffee as a sort of tonic, an elixir capable of delivering both strength and inspiration. He enjoyed it luxuriously. An impatient Vledder stood next to his desk. DeKok looked up at him and savored his restlessness along with his coffee.

"What's the matter my boy," he asked in mock surprise, "haven't had your coffee yet?"

Vledder snorted.

"Coffee, coffee," he growled ill tempered, "always coffee first. The Commissaris said that you had to report to him *immediately!* Not after an extensive coffee break." He made an obvious irritated gesture. "Furthermore," he continued, "I'd have thought that you would find the news of Bogaard's escape from the hospital rather important."

Comfortably DeKok continued to sip his coffee.

"Listen to me," he said, placing his mug in front of him, "one does not escape from a hospital. A hospital is not a prison. At most one could conclude that Frank Bogaard did not appreciate the medical facilities available to him."

"It's the same thing. In any case, Frank jumped out of the window and disappeared down the street in his pajamas. The crew of a patrol car saw him this morning, near the Leiden Woods. A man in night clothes does draw some attention, after all."

"And?"

"They took him in the car and delivered him here, at the Warmoes Street, downstairs."

DeKok looked surprised.

"Here? But why didn't take him straight back to the hospital?"

"He didn't want to go. He most emphatically did not want to return to the hospital, unless he had spoken with you first."

"Me?"

"Yes, he's downstairs. He's waiting for you."

With one last, giant swallow, DeKok drained his mug and stood up.

"Come on," he said, "let's go and hear what Frank has to say."

Vledder looked at him in astonishment.

"But, . . . eh, what about the Commissaris?"

DeKok pointed at the large clock on the wall.

"The Commissaris has no time for me, right now."

"No time?"

DeKok shook his head.

"It's ten o'clock. The Commissaris is having coffee."

* * *

He had been taken to one of the interrogation rooms and that is where they found him. Frank Bogaard offered a shivering, shaking picture of human misery, as he leaned against the radiator in the corner. He looked ridiculous in a wrinkled suit, left over from a drowning, and an old uniform overcoat from a sergeant, now since long retired. A friendly constable had taken pity on him and issued whatever clothing could be found, because he was cold in his pajamas, as well as a result of the symptoms of withdrawal. But it did not help much. He was still shivering.

Frank Bogaard could not get warm. He shook and shivered. Sadly, knees pulled up under his chin, he barely looked up as DeKok and Vledder entered the room.

DeKok took a chair and straddled it backward, his arms resting on the back of the chair. He had an indeterminate feeling that the seriously ill young man in front of him, was the key to the riddle created by Nanette. He just did not know, yet, how the key would fit. It was still all so vague, so mysterious, so, he looked for the word and found it, so ethereal.

"Why didn't you stay in bed? It's rather dumb to start roaming the street in pajamas, especially in the middle of the night." DeKok's tone of voice was friendly, confidential. Soft, like a caring nurse. "If you had wanted to speak to me, I would have been glad to come."

Frank looked up. It was as if he just now noticed the presence of the two detectives. He looked from Vledder to DeKok, a hunted look in his eyes.

"Where is Nanette?"

DeKok shrugged his shoulders.

"I don't know. Nanette has disappeared. I told you so, yesterday."

The young man flicked a quick tongue along dry lips.

"Yes," he said tonelessly, "you told me she had disappeared. Nanette has disappeared, you told me. She's . . ." He kept repeating the same phrase, over and over, with slight variations. Monotonous, as if trapped in a single thought.

Suddenly he seemed to free himself from the spell of his own words. His face gained some expression, the dullness, the apparent lack of intelligence slowly disappeared and changed into an expression of fear. He gripped DeKok's arms.

"You must find her, Mr. DeKok," He said quickly and in a hoarse voice. "As soon as possible. You must find her. You must."

DeKok gave him a penetrating look.

"Why?" he asked sharply, "so that she can supply you with your next fix?"

Bogaard's mouth fell open. Then he started to grin idiotically, nervously.

"How did you know that Nanette . . . that she was my . . .?"

". . . Your supplier," completed DeKok. Then he added: "Since yesterday."

Bogaard released DeKok's arms, turned, waved his arms in the air and sank down on a chair.

"B-But then you must understand," he stuttered, "y-you must understand that she is in grave danger. Every minute is important. You mustn't loose a moment. You must find her, before . . . before it's too late."

DeKok rubbed the back of his nose with his pinky.

"Too late?"

Bogaard's face contorted in fury.

"Yes," he screamed, "too late! There are no more ruthless people than drug dealers. You must know that. It's scum, all of them. Blood suckers, poisonous snakes, hyenas, vultures."

DeKok pulled on his lower lip.

"Who," he asked, "delivered the drugs to Nanette that she, in turn, delivered to you?"

Frank Bogaard shrugged his shoulders.

"I don't know," he answered morosely.

"Did she never discuss it with you?"

"No, never."

"And you never asked her?"

"No!"

DeKok sighed.

"You must have heard her a mention a name, sometimes."

Frank hesitated momentarily.

"No!"

"Think hard."

"*No!*" he screamed it out.

DeKok pressed his lips together. He just knew the young man was lying. He felt that he knew more than he wanted to say. Slowly DeKok rose, gripped Bogaard by the lapels of his coat and lifted him out of the chair.

"What did you pay Nanette, for the stuff?"

"Nothing."

DeKok took a firmer grip and pulled the young man closer.

"What," he asked intensely, "did you pay her for the stuff?"

Bogaard swallowed.

"Nothing. Really, I've never paid her a single solitary nickel for it."

DeKok's eyebrows started their dangerous ripple.

"Why not?" The tone was incredulous.

"She didn't want any money."

"What did she want?"

"Nothing," he screamed, "she wanted nothing."

DeKok snorted contemptuously.

"Oh, yes. Nanette, sweet angel of mercy, distributes free dope among the poor, the tired and the huddled masses." His voice dripped with sarcasm. "Was it mercy? Or was it something else? Love for instance, pure love for cousin Frank. Was that it?"

Bogaard turned his head and did not answer.

DeKok was getting angry.

"Was that it?" he pressed. "Love?" He pronounced it like a curse.

Frank's eyes were red rimmed. The eyeballs started to glaze. Hot tears dribbled on his cheeks, dripped on the hairy back of DeKok's hand. It seemed to burn like drops of hot metal.

DeKok's grip became less tight. He looked in the pale, unhealthy face of young Bogaard, looked at the tears, the soft, slightly weak facial features and suddenly noticed how much he and his sister Kristel had in common. It made him less angry.

"Sit down," he said softly. "How about a cup of coffee?"

Bogaard pulled his coat straight and sank down in the chair.

"I'd rather have a cigarette."

DeKok presented an opened pack.

"Sometimes I may appear a little less friendly," he apologized. "Not because I want to be, you understand, but because it's my job."

A trace of a smile fled over the tired face of Frank Bogaard. He lifted his right arm, causing the long sleeve of the old uniform coat to fall back to near his elbow and accepted a cigarette with shaking fingers.

DeKok provided a light.

"I want to know," he continued calmly, "why Nanette disappeared. Perhaps, just maybe, I can then discover where she disappeared to. You, see," he explained further, "I have a feeling that the two are connected, that they are very closely linked. The one cannot be excluded from the other."

He paused briefly. Then lit a cigarette himself. He seldom smoked, but used cigarettes as a weapon, as in the case of Wielen, or to help create a confidential atmosphere,

95

as in this case. Slowly he blew smoke to the ceiling. Only Vledder noticed he did not inhale.

"Mr. Bogaard, an extremely important question. Think! Was Nanette a poisonous snake, a vulture, a hyena, or an angel?"

Frank did not react at once. He lowered his head. He thought about it, was obviously looking for the right way to compose his answer.

"Most people," he said finally, slowly, "are often all those things at the same time, a repulsive sight, an incomplete composition with strange, shrill dissonants, shades of good and evil."

"And what about Nanette?"

Frank pulled deeply on his cigarette. He looked at DeKok through a heavy cloud of bluish smoke. His eyes narrowed slightly.

"Nanette," he said with an unpleasant grin, "Nanette, is a poisonous snake in the shape of an angel."

DeKok rubbed his hands over his broad face.

"An almost classical disguise," he said with a trace of sarcasm. "Very old. Been used from the very beginning." He made a slow, lazy gesture. "The daughters of Eve have, apparently, little originality."

"But the apple became morphine," grinned Bogaard bitterly.

DeKok looked at him for a long time, silent. The bitter remark had touched him. After a while he stood up and pushed his chair back.

"We'll have you taken back to the hospital, Mr. Bogaard. But you must promise not to indulge in repeated nightly excursions. The doctors don't like it. It's also not conducive to your health." He placed a concerned hand on Frank's slender, shaking shoulder. "You must remember that you have very little leeway left for experimentation," he concluded.

Bogaard looked up at him.

"What do you mean by that?"

"Your health is more undermined than even you can suspect, Mr. Bogaard. A second nightly escapade may very well be fatal."

"Fatal?"

DeKok nodded with a grave face.

"I would like to see you stay alive."

Nonchalantly, Bogaard shrugged his shoulders.

"Why?" he asked.

"A young, promising author ...," DeKok gestured vaguely.

Frank sighed deeply.

"You mock me."

DeKok shook his head.

"No, not me," he answered sharply. "Not me. I don't mock you, but you mock yourself. You're playing with your life, and that of Nanette."

"Me?"

"Yes, you!" exclaimed DeKok with emphasis. "Every moment is valuable, you said. That remains true. Frank Bogaard, who supplied Nanette with heroin?"

"I ... eh, I don't know."

"You *do* know!"

The young man's eyes filled with tears.

"Really, Mr. DeKok," he begged, "please believe me. I don't know. I really don't know. In passing, almost by accident, I've just heard her once mention a name in connection with dope. Just once. She spoke of a Brother Laurens. It just slipped out. When I asked her who that was, she laughed. She never told me."

DeKok raked his thick, gray hair with his fingers. "Brother Laurens! Who is Brother Laurens?"

9

Commissaris Buitendam, the tall, stately chief of the station in the Warmoes Street, frowned perplexed as DeKok, busily and nervously entered his large office.

It was a pose, almost a game. The Commissaris knew it. DeKok knew that the Commissaris knew it. Neither fooled the other. They had known each other for too long. Their association started in the almost forgotten past. Over the years the polite phrases had been twisted and modulated until they resembled a comedy, a farce, performed with utter seriousness by both of them.

"You wanted to see me immediately?"

The Commissaris smiled thinly.

"Yes, about an hour and a half ago," he answered.

DeKok hung his head in shame.

"Sir, it is unforgivable. But I didn't want to disturb you while you were having your coffee."

The Commissaris coughed.

"That is very considerate of you, DeKok."

"At your service, sir."

The Commissaris coughed again.

"But I go so far as to presume that the coffee could not have been the only reason?"

DeKok shook his gray head and took a chair.

"With your permission?"

"But of course, please sit down, DeKok, and tell me all about it."

"I was engaged in an investigation."

"Connected with that girl who disappeared?"

"Indeed."

The Commissaris searched among the papers on his desk.

"That's what I wanted to discuss with you. I read the telex message, the APB. It must be here, somewhere. What was the name again?"

"Nanette Bogaard."

"Oh, yes. Nanette Bogaard. Here it is." The Commissaris waved a copy of the APB in the air. "What's the situation. Are you making progress?"

"It is rather a confusing story. I have to confess honestly that I don't understand it at all, at all. The how and the why of her disappearance is still a complete mystery."

"Clues?"

Shyly, embarrassed, DeKok scratched the back of his neck.

"Too many, way too many. That's the difficulty. The further I get, the more I have the feeling that I'm being led astray. That I am getting farther away from the solution. It may sound contradictory, but that's the case."

The Commissaris nodded his understanding.

"What about a release to the press? The radio? Or even TV?"

DeKok made a negating gesture with both hands.

"No, rather not. At least, not yet. You know how that goes. One such release breaks all floodgates. A veritable avalanche of tips, most, if not all, false, or misleading. One person saw her in the North, another in the South, some saw her in Paris, or God knows where. There is no end to that. Only if I've really reached a dead end, if there's no progress to be made any other way, then, and only then, should we consider that approach."

Slowly the Commissaris nodded agreement.

"Have you any idea where she could be?"

"Not the slightest."

"How much longer do you think you'll need to find her. I mean, if the D.A. asks me . . ."

DeKok shrugged.

"If she's still alive . . ."

The Commissaris gave him a searching look.

"What do you mean?"

"Exactly what I'm saying. If she's still alive. I cannot rule out the possibility that Nanette Bogaard is no more. I'm almost certain that she is dead, killed, murdered."

"Murdered?"

DeKok rubbed his face with both hands. An infinitely weary gesture.

"Yes, murdered. It's really the only reasonable explanation for her sudden disappearance."

Thoughtfully the Commissaris looked at his subordinate.

"Murder," he said finally, "murder requires a motive."

DeKok nodded.

"A motive *and* a body. But as long as we haven't found Nanette Bogaard, dead or alive, we can't be much more positive. For the time being it seems best that I continue to follow all clues. Expand the investigations. We'll find out soon enough where that'll lead us."

"All right, keep me informed."

"But of course."

101

Both stood up and walked toward the door.

"Was . . . eh, is Nanette a good looking girl?"

DeKok made an awkward gesture.

"Yes, according to modern ideas, yes, she's beautiful. But Rubens would not exactly have laid awake nights, over her."

The telephone rang. Smiling, the Commissaris turned, picked it up and listened.

"It's for you."

DeKok accepted the receiver and recognized the voice of antique dealer Grevelen. He was talking to an excited voice in the background. Trying to calm it down.

"Hallo."

"Inspector DeKok?"

"Yes."

"Mr. DeKok, I request you to come here immediately. Now, at once. I'm at the shop on the Mirror's Canal."

"Why at once? What's the matter?"

Grevelen could be heard to swallow.

"There's a man here who demands the painting. You know, the somber nude."

"What!?"

"Yes, he claims that the painting is his property. Somebody must have stolen it from his house, a few days ago, complete with frame and all."

DeKok thought quickly.

"Don't let him go. Keep him there."

"Who?"

"That man, of course. I'll come at once."

DeKok threw the receiver down and ran from the office. The Commissaris looked after him, astonished. DeKok waved good bye.

In the corridor, nearing the stairs, he started to call for Vledder.

"Vledder, Vledder, Vledder!"

His deep bass voice echoed through the building.

* * *

Wringing his hands, the old antique dealer, Grevelen, was waiting on the stoop in front of his shop. Small, red spots of excitement colored his lean, hollow cheeks.

"I'm so glad you're here," he said, relieved. "The man is crazy, furious." He laughed nervously. "He wanted to take the painting with him. Just like that. He cursed like all the devils from hell when I told him he had to wait for you."

"Where is he?"

"Still inside. I kept him for you. One of my staff guards the door."

DeKok nodded approvingly.

"Excellent, really excellent. We'll see what he has to say for himself."

Followed by Vledder and the scared antiquarian, DeKok entered the shop: big, broad, imposing, forceful. Fleetingly Vledder thought about the proverbial bull in the china shop.

An older man was standing toward the back of the shop. Next to him was an alert, young man in the traditional gray coat of a warehouse worker. DeKok took another look at the older man. A well preserved fifty, or so, he estimated. A tanned face, grayish at the temples. The man was elegantly dressed, perhaps a little too youthful, in a light blue suit of a particular modern cut. In his lapel was a small white rose as a boutonniere.

"This is unheard of! Ridiculous!"

DeKok halted in front of the man. He stood in a particularly insolent manner. Legs apart, searchingly, the head slightly cocked. A faint smile on his face, playful, happy, almost mocking.

"My name is DeKok. That's DeKok with . . . eh, kay-oh-kay. This is my colleague Vledder. I think you have already had the pleasure of Mr. Grevelen's acquaintance?"

The man murmured something that could be taken as a greeting. Then he pointed toward the wall.

"My painting," he blurted out, excitedly. "Stolen!"

DeKok ignored the remark. Quasi surprised he looked at the man.

"I do not believe," he said with sweet sarcasm, "that I have had the pleasure of making your acquaintance."

The man sighed.

"Staaten. Stockbroker."

DeKok made him the recipient of his sunniest smile.

"My pleasure, Mr. Staaten. So you're the man who claims that the painting, over there, is your property."

"Indeed yes. My property. It has been stolen from my house."

"Stolen?"

"Yes."

"And have you reported the theft?"

"No."

"Why not?"

"Simply because I had not yet discovered the theft. You see, the painting was in my house on the Emperor's Canal. Because of a set of circumstances, I have not been there for the last few days."

DeKok nodded understandingly.

"Burglary?"

"No, no burglary. It was just gone. Just the painting. When I came home, late last night, I immediately noticed the empty spot in my living room. I missed it at once. I am very attached to the painting."

DeKok looked up, past the antique pistols and rested his gaze on the painting.

"It is exceptionally beautiful," he said. Then, after a short pause, he continued: "How did you know so quickly that the painting was here, in this shop?"

Staaten hesitated monetarily.

"Somebody called me," he said finally.

"Who?"

"That . . . eh, that I don't know."

DeKok looked at him with sharpened interest.

"Strange, don't you think?"

The man shrugged his shoulders.

"I did not really think about it. No, I did not realize that. Shortly after I discovered the disappearance of the painting, somebody called. A man. He wanted to know if I had sold my Nanette."

"Your Nanette?"

"The painting. The girl who was the model, her name is Nanette."

DeKok rubbed his flat hand over his face. He felt instinctively that he should not keep asking questions much longer. The environment, the place, it was not conducive to a proper interrogation. Especially he thought it less advisable to elicit a specific confession from the broker in the presence of the dealer and his assistant.

"You understand, Mr. Staaten," he continued with a winning smile, "that we cannot hand the painting over to you, just like that. That's simply impossible. First, at the very least, we'll have to investigate this rather mysterious theft."

The detective turned to the antiquary.

"I assume that you bought the painting in the normal, legal manner and that the purchase has been registered in your books?"

Grevelen looked strangely at DeKok and then nodded.

"But, of course. Certainly," he said with emphasis. "It has and I have the name, I'll say, the name of the seller has been recorded. Completely, including the number of the passport which was used as identification. I personally bought the painting."

"May I see the register a moment, please?"

"But, of course, I'll fetch it at once."

The old man walked toward the back of the store, to his office, and returned within seconds with a large book. He handed it to DeKok with a meaningful glance in his eyes.

"Please look on page seventeen," he said.

DeKok opened the book and turned pages. It was an exceptionally neat record. He had seen few like it. The purchases and sales were all noted, dated, and recorded in a minuscule, but very legible handwriting. The dealer seemed to have a penchant for detail.

On page seventeen DeKok ran his finger along the entries. Almost at the bottom of the page he found it: *Painting, measuring 40 x 32 inches in gilded frame with scroll work and arabesques, female figure, nude, on red brocade sofa, purchased from . . .*

Surprised, DeKok looked up.

"Who," he asked the broker, "is Ronald Staaten?"

The broker's mouth fell open.

"*Ronald* Staaten?" he asked.

DeKok nodded.

With the back of his hand the broker wiped along his dry lips. Meanwhile he looked suspiciously at DeKok. Finally he said:

"Ronald, Ronald is my son."

10

DeKok leaned both elbows on his desk. He looked at the stockbroker from across his folded hands. He noticed a worried look on the tanned face.

"Please, don't consider this a formal arrest, Mr. Staaten. On the contrary, I have merely asked you to the station in order to help the police with its inquiries. I want to know a little more about you and the painting. Also, you'll admit, the strange behavior of your son, in regard to you and the painting, requires a certain amount of explanation."

Staaten nodded slowly.

"I understand. However, I don't think that I'm the one to give you much clarification."

DeKok gave him a winning smile.

"At least we can try, together, and see how far we'll get. That is, if you're prepared to cooperate."

"Cooperate? To what end?"

"Well, we can reasonably assume that your son, Ronald, is responsible for the theft of the painting from your house on the Emperor's Canal. The proof for this, you'll agree, is virtually incontrovertible: no signs of breaking and entering, the sale to the antique dealer, it's all rather straight forward. But I assume that you are not prepared to file a formal complaint against your son, for the theft that is. You're not prepared to request formal prosecution, are you?"

Staaten shook his head vehemently.

"I'll say! Out of the question! The very thought! Ronald is my only child. After the death of my dear wife, he's all I have left."

DeKok nodded understanding.

"Exactly. As far as that is concerned, there is nothing for you to worry about, at least from me. I mean, if you don't file a complaint, I can't touch your son. Officially no crime has then been committed. But I am nevertheless very interested in the motive. I assume that you, as the father, are as intrigued as I am, Mr. Staaten. . . . Why would your son steal the painting and then sell it to an antique dealer? Was he in financial difficulties?"

The broker shrugged his shoulders.

"Ronald enjoys a generous allowance. And if he does need something extra, he has only to ask. I've never yet refused him anything."

"An enviable position for a son," smiled DeKok.

Staaten showed a weary smile.

"I can afford it."

The gray sleuth pushed his chair a little backward and stretched his legs. He would have loved to place them on the desk, as he sometimes did. But, in the presence of a third person, he resisted the urge.

"You like paintings?" he asked.

"Yes, I'm a collector and a connoisseur," nodded Staaten. "I own," he continued, "a considerable collection."

"At the Emperor's Canal?"

"Yes, primarily."

110

DeKok pushed his chair forward again. He leaned toward the broker. His sharp gaze was alert to every reaction.

"But why would Ronald take just *that* particular painting?"

Staaten stretched his neck and placed two fingers inside his collar, as if trying to get some extra air.

"That . . . eh, that I don't know."

DeKok stared at him searchingly.

"Really, Mr. Staaten," he said gently, "you really don't know why Ronald selected just *Nanette*, of all your paintings?"

Staaten placed a hand in front of his eyes and rubbed the corners of his eyes with a thumb and index finger.

"You're forcing me to say something, I'd rather not say."

DeKok shook his head.

"I don't force you to do anything. You're just afraid to face the truth. That's all. You're son picked exactly the painting that meant most to you. Am I right?"

The stockbroker sighed.

"You're absolutely right," he said finally, almost toneless and expressionless. "Ronald wanted to hurt me. Punish me."

He paused, lost in thought.

"He's not a bad boy, Mr. DeKok, not at all. He's just rather sentimental, sensitive, like his mother. He was very much attached to her, a strong bonding, you understand. He was always more her son than mine. I didn't mind, too much, although I would have liked to see him a bit more independent, a bit more manly."

Again he paused. Then he continued:

"After my wife's death I feared that Ronald would grow farther and farther away from me. Fortunately that did not happen. On the contrary. Over time we grew very close. There was a bond between us, based on mutual friendship and respect. Almost an ideal father-son relationship. I could not have asked for more. Really."

He sighed again. A weary sigh.

"But recently there were some difficulties."

"Recently?"

"Yes."

"Why?"

Staaten did not answer.

Slowly DeKok rose and came from behind his desk. He felt a certain amount of pity for the successful stockbroker. The obvious blue of his suit. The playful rose in the button hole . . .

"Why," he pressed, "were there recent difficulties between you and your son?"

Staaten bent his head.

"I . . . eh, I was planning to marry again," he whispered.

"Remarry?"

"Yes."

"And . . . Ronald was against it? Did not approve?"

The broker responded violently. With an abrupt movement he turned and looked DeKok full in the face. His cheeks turned red and his eyes spat fire.

"It's not up to Ronald to approve, or disapprove," he said sharply, "I'm a free man, he's neither my guardian, nor my conscience. I'm my own boss and fully competent to evaluate the consequences of my own actions. I'm not exactly senile!"

His tone changed.

"Listen, Mr. DeKok," he continued, calmer, "I have very dear and fond memories of my wife. But she's dead. The dead cannot rule the living. I'm fifty five years old, healthy and virile. In any case, virile enough to be able to count on a number of happy years with Nanette."

DeKok arched his eyebrows in his own, inimitable manner.

"Nanette . . . Nanette Bogaard?"

"Yes."

"The girl who modeled for the nude?"

"Indeed."

"Oh."

Staaten moved restlessly in his chair.

"Do you . . . eh, do you know her?"

DeKok wiped his hand over his mouth.

"That's difficult to say," he said, hesitatingly, "I've never met her in person. Yet, I've the feeling that I know her very well, indeed."

"I don't understand," said the broker, looking intently at the detective.

DeKok did not answer at once. He paced up and down the detective room for a while and thought about his answer. It was difficult to come up with the correct phrasing. He could not decide.

DeKok halted in front of the window. He looked carefully at the broker from a distance. A cool evaluation. In his own way, Staaten was a handsome man, he thought. Certainly the type which would be attractive to a young girl. He could very well imagine how that could have happened. Nanette and the charming, debonair stockbroker. Probably they met in *Ye Three Roses*, while he was replenishing his boutonniere. It was on his way. The Stock Market was close by. One thing led to another. DeKok raked his fingers through his gray hair. Was this man responsible for Nanette's disappearance? Or perhaps the son was responsible?

DeKok came closer.

"How old is your son?" he asked.

Bristling, Staaten rose from his chair. His eyes narrowed and his lips were pressed together until they formed a thin line across the bottom part of his angry face.

"Ronald," he said, almost venomously, "Ronald is twenty five years old and I know exactly what you're going to say, what you're thinking, as far as age is concerned, Nanette could have been my daughter."

Reproachfully DeKok shook his head.

"Please sit down, Mr. Staaten," he said calmly, soothingly. "Why do you get so excited? I don't condemn you at all, at all. On the contrary, I congratulate you, I wish you all possible happiness. That's why I hope that I will be able to find Nanette for you, as soon as possible."

The broker's eyes blinked. His face assumed an expression of genuine amazement.

"Find Nanette, you said?"

"Indeed, yes. I said find. Nanette Bogaard, you should know, seems to have disappeared."

"Disappeared?"

"Yes."

"Since when?"

"Since Thursday. She left the flower shop around three in the afternoon and nobody has seen her since."

A silence followed this statement.

It was obviously difficult for the broker to absorb the statement made by DeKok. All color had drained from his face. He suddenly looked years older. A tired, worried businessman. After a long while he looked up.

"She left no message?"

DeKok sighed.

"You don't seem to grasp the situation, Mr. Staaten. Nanette is gone, disappeared and . . . I don't think she went voluntarily." He paused. "I'm afraid," he continued, "that something has happened to her, you understand? Something serious."

Staaten smiled sadly to himself.

"No," he said with a weary sigh, "no, nothing has happened to Nanette. Nothing serious, I mean. She's just fled. Escaped from the consequences. She had promised to marry me." He shook his head, as if to clear his thoughts. "I should never have asked her. I should never have forced the promise from her." He sighed again. "She didn't want to hurt my feelings, that's all, she didn't want to refuse me. That's why she agreed. It isn't her fault. I, I should have been wiser."

DeKok's eyebrows formed an interesting shape. It was too bad that Staaten was not in the mood to appreciate it.

"You think that she's disappeared in order to escape a promise of marriage?"

"Yes, absolutely. There is no other explanation. Nanette . . . She has simply realized the age difference and got scared." He smiled a bitter smile, full of irony. "After all, I'm not exactly what you would call a spring chicken," he concluded.

All this time young Vledder had leaned against a far wall. Almost unnoticed. He had listened carefully to the conversation between DeKok and the stockbroker. Not a single word, no inflection, had escaped him. Slowly a theory had formed in the back of his mind. Slowly it became more concrete, took on more substance. He looked at his old mentor and waited for an opening.

DeKok saw his eager look and nodded permission. He walked over to the window and gave his pupil room to continue the interrogation of Staaten.

Vledder came closer.

"How had you envisioned the marriage between you and Nanette, Mr. Staaten. Were you planning to arrange for a pre-nuptial agreement, or something like that? After all, you're a wealthy man. Were you planning to marry Nanette under the community property laws, or were there going to be certain safeguards?"

Confused, the broker looked at Vledder.

"Well, ... eh, to tell you the truth, I ... eh, I've never really thought about it."

"Perhaps not you, but others?"

The broker's face became expressionless.

"You mean ...?"

"Ronald is your only son, your sole heir."

Staaten reacted strongly.

"What are you trying to imply?"

His voice was sharp and challenging.

Vledder smiled faintly.

"Based on your reaction," he said calmly, "you know exactly what I'm trying to suggest, Mr. Staaten. In case of a marriage between you and Nanette, Ronald would be the injured party, in a manner of speaking. At the very least he would lose a great part of his future wealth, his inheritance. If we're looking for a motive connected with Nanette's disappearance, then your son ..."

Wildly gesticulating, the broker jumped to his feet. In a blind, uncontrollable rage he took his tormentor by the throat and pressed down on Vledder's windpipe. It was a complete surprise attack. Vledder had not expected it, nor had DeKok. For a moment Vledder was too surprised to

116

move. Then he came into action. The elder Staaten was no match for the young, athletic Vledder. With a quick movement, almost a blur, he took hold of the stockbroker and pushed him away.

DeKok came closer, upset. He pushed Vledder aside and took the shaking broker by the arm and led him to another room. There he placed him on a chair and gave him a glass of water.

"You must control yourself, Mr. Staaten," he said sternly and reprovingly. "My colleague only made a suggestion, a *reasonable* suggestion. It was not an accusation."

He pressed the glass of water on him.

"Here, have another sip. When you have calmed down, you're going home and you ask your son to contact us. I have to put a few official questions to him."

The broker looked at the old Inspector.

"Are you going to arrest him?"

DeKok rubbed his hand over his chin.

"Why should I? Because he killed Nanette?"

11

Vledder stood in front of the mirror and looked at the red streaks on his neck. DeKok stood behind him, looking over his shoulder.

"How is it, my boy?" he asked, concerned. "Does it hurt?"

Vledder shook his head.

"No, no, it doesn't hurt," he answered, irritated, "not much, anyway. It just looks terrible, worse than it is. And so visible. So tonight I'll have to explain it all to Celine. She cannot help but notice."

"And," said DeKok, slightly mocking, "she's *so* concerned."

Vledder turned abruptly.

"Yes," he said sharply. "Do you find that strange? Celine is concerned for me. She isn't at all happy about my assignment with you, here at Homicide. She's heard, from colleagues, that you have a habit of getting involved with all sorts of strange cases. She's afraid."

DeKok snorted.

"Some colleagues are just like old women. They talk too much. But ... if you rather have another partner ... that ... eh, that can be arranged."

Vledder's face changed under the influence of conflicting emotions.

"No, no, DeKok," he said, shocked. "I don't mean it that way. I don't want another partner. On the contrary, I couldn't have found a better partner, nobody I'd rather work with."

"You flatter me, my boy," grinned DeKok, "indeed, you flatter me."

Vledder rubbed his neck again.

"Staaten has a considerable amount of strength in those skinny fingers. Dammit, it was like a steel trap. If we ever find out that Nanette was strangled, we'll know who the perpetrator was."

"And I rather thought that you favored his son as a suspect?"

"True, I do. So far he's the only one with a clear motive. Ronald was interested in making Nanette disappear. You know," he said suddenly, "Staaten realized immediately how strong that motive could be. How it literally jumped out. That's why he became so angry."

DeKok nodded.

"He reacted from a sense of guilt."

"Guilt?"

"Yes, guilt. If you ask me, Staaten felt guilty about his amorous relationship with Nanette. Felt guilty about the marriage proposal. He felt it as a sin. Something contrary to public opinion. Against the customs and mores of society. His attitude during the interrogation points to that as well. He was constantly in a sort of aggressive adversary position. As if we were accusing him, as if we were passing a moral judgement. He defended his relations with Nanette although there was no reason to do so at all, at all. Neither you, nor I, even hinted at it."

DeKok paused, as if gathering his thoughts. Then he continued his impromptu summation:

"But his sharpest reaction came later, his most aggressive behavior was reserved for when you pointed out that his relationship with Nanette could be seen as detrimental to the welfare of his son. That his son might conceive of murder, rather than accept Nanette as his step-mother. Intellectually he had no defense, no reasonable argument. That's why he attacked you."

DeKok remain silent. For a while he stared at nothing in particular.

"It is always ... eh, difficult," he continued slowly, "perhaps even dangerous, to try and analyze someone's reactions and to use that analysis to come to a conclusion. Especially when one is not familiar with the background. It becomes mere speculation. But, in my personal view, Staaten's attack on you was a sort of confession, an admission of guilt. In his heart, in his deepest thoughts, he has already considered your suggestion and believes it to be possible."

He raised a finger into the air.

"You must keep in mind that Staaten is an intelligent man. Please note, a stockbroker, someone very capable of weighing a number of different factors and to draw a conclusion. The right conclusion, more often than not, or he would not have been able to amass such a fortune."

Looking at his finger, as if surprised to find it there, he used it to rub the bridge of his nose.

"He must have considered all the pros and cons of his intended marriage to Nanette and his son must have been an important part of his deliberations. Therefore, when you offered the possibility that Ronald might have a valid motive for killing Nanette, I half expected him to counter that suggestion with a superior, or arrogant smile, as something unthinkable, off the wall, if you like. But he didn't do that, you understand. He did not reject your suggestion. He reacted, as he did, quickly, furiously, guilt ridden."

Vledder looked at his mentor with wide eyes.

"Yes, yes, I understand," he answered, shaken. "Staaten did not ridicule the suggestion, because he's very well aware that his son is capable of murder."

DeKok nodded slowly.

"Indeed, that's the way I see it. And we'll have to keep that in mind, as we progress."

Suddenly Vledder laughed loudly.

"I can't help it," he grinned, "but I think it's a strange case, all in all."

"Why?"

"Well, we run from one hint to another, slowly we're convinced we have to watch everything and everybody, see suspects behind every corner, hold long, philosophical conversations about all sort of possibilities, while . . . if you think about it, nothing has really happened, yet."

Surprised, DeKok looked at him.

"A girl has disappeared, remember?"

"Well, yes, but is that a crime?"

"Listen to me, son." DeKok sounded resigned. "Of course, theoretically, there's always the chance that we'll find Nanette unharmed. Of course. But the longer this investigation takes, the longer she's gone, the less I believe in it. We're more than a day on the case and have been unable to get any proof of a *living* Nanette. On the contrary, we've found quite a few indications to suggest that a number of people might be interested in a *dead* Nanette."

DeKok sighed deeply.

"It sounds sinister, but that's the way it is."

Vledder tried to frown but, as usual unable to make his eyebrows cooperate, he settled for creasing his forehead.

"You said 'a number' of people. Plural. But, apart from Ronald Staaten, I don't see anybody else with a real motive. There are more, you think?"

"Most certainly. For instance, have you forgotten Brother Laurens? Who's that, then?"

"You refer, I presume, to the name mentioned by Frank Bogaard. According to him, he had heard the name in connection with drugs. Nanette had mentioned it, he said."

"Exactly, because of the painting business he's moved a bit to the back burner. But I'm still very much interested in Brother Laurens. You see, he could also be a possible suspect."

"A possible suspect," scoffed Vledder, "you don't even know who it is."

"That's not necessary. I mean, even without knowing Brother Laurens, we can come to a number of interesting, almost obvious, conclusions."

"Such as?"

DeKok sat on the corner of his desk. His relatively short legs swung back and forth. Amused he looked at young Vledder, a gentle smile on his craggy face.

"Think, my boy," he said, "think hard!"

"What is there to think about?" asked Vledder, irritated. We don't even know if 'Laurens' is a first name, or a surname."

Approvingly, DeKok nodded.

"Very good," he said encouragingly, "very good. Both are possible. Indeed. We're only guessing at the spelling. It could be Lawrence, or Lorentz, or Laurens, the more common, Dutch spelling. But what about the concept

'Brother'? Where do we, normally, use the appellation 'Brother' in front of the name?"

Vledder grimaced.

"A Brother of the Lord, in a religious sense, or a monk. Maybe a member of a fraternity, or a union. Perhaps even a family relationship. 'Bro' maybe. Mockingly, or deprecatingly . . . eh, I don't know."

DeKok shook his head.

"I was thinking of a different connection altogether."

"Not religious. No other kind of brotherhood?"

"No."

Suddenly Vledder's face cleared.

"I have it. As in medicine. Of course, a nurse is so often referred to as 'sister', especially with all the English influence in the language. Now that there are more and more male nurses, people refer to them as 'brother'."

"Excellent. And what, if I may express it that way, is the occupational abode of such a brother? Such a male nurse."

"Usually a hospital. Or a sanitarium, or rest home."

DeKok pushed his lower lip forward.

"Now think of drugs."

"Dammit, yes!" exclaimed Vledder enthusiastically. "You're right! A hospital, drugs, morphine! Of course! Brother Laurens, that's it! He's got to be Nanette's supplier. A male nurse. It's the only way. Really, DeKok, it's the missing link. Brother Laurens steals the morphine in whatever hospital he works, passes it on to Nanette, who supplies Frank, to help him with his writer's block."

DeKok laughed at the enthusiastic tone and excitement displayed by Vledder. He raised a cautioning finger in the air.

"As usual," he grinned, "you're too eager to trot, too soon. Therefore you're overlooking a number of important questions."

"Questions?"

"Just think a moment . . . Why should Brother Laurens deliver drugs to Nanette? Why should he run the risk?"

Vledder stared at his mentor with a questioning look on his face.

"Why?" he asked finally.

"Yes, why? You forget that Nanette wasn't interested in money. She couldn't care less about money, or so we've been told. Frank Bogaard told us that she didn't want any money from him. And I believe him. Nanette supplied him for free, gratis."

DeKok lowered his arm.

"How could Nanette afford that?" he continued. "I mean, financially. As far as we know she had no money of her own. Her sole capital was her share in the flower shop. And as you'll remember, Kristel was the financial manager. So, no matter what, Nanette would be unable to pay Brother Laurens. She simply didn't have the funds. But yet, . . . but, yet she supplied Frank regularly. Why?"

"I understand." Vledder nodded in agreement. "You're telling me that Brother Laurens was persuaded some other way. Had a different reason for accommodating Nanette. Money wasn't the motive."

"Exactly. I repeat my question: Why did he supply Nanette? Was he in love with her? A love she exploited, or was Nanette blackmailing him?"

"Blackmail?"

DeKok nodded. His face was serious.

"Yes. If we consider the physical condition of Frank Bogaard, his physical deterioration, we can only conclude that Nanette has been supplying him for some time. At least a year, or more. Something must have compelled our Brother Laurens to continue to deliver considerable quantities of morphine to her. You have to remember, that something like that, over a period of time, not even a very long time, becomes more and more dangerous. The chance of discovery increases with every theft. But yet he persisted. Apparently Nanette had a very strong hold over Brother Laurens. I only know one explanation for such a strong hold over a person: Blackmail!"

DeKok made a careful gesture. He paused, then continued:

"But that doesn't explain everything. Not by a long shot. First we have to track down Brother Laurens. Then we have to determine what Nanette used as blackmail, if that's what it is. But of one thing I'm certain. Brother Laurens, too, had a good reason, an excellent motive, to kill Nanette."

Grinning, Vledder shook his head.

"All in all, I keep thinking that this is a very strange case." He chuckled and said: "We don't even have a corpse, but the list of suspects grows exponentially."

DeKok did not answer. He could be infuriating that way. Vledder secretly wished he could ignore things and people as well as DeKok did, at times.

Meanwhile DeKok thought. He was not at all happy with the case of Nanette. It was a bit too unorthodox, too peculiar. He was wondering how to proceed, where to turn next. Young Vledder was right, it was a strange case.

A girl had disappeared. A beautiful, young girl. Suddenly she was gone. Just like that, on a rainy day in July. And nobody had seen her. *Why* had she disappeared? *Who* was she? Or, perhaps even more important, *how* was she?

Carefree, according to cousin Kristel, with a special interest in art and literature.

Wielen, friend and journalist, described her most enthusiastically as a wild daisy from *Ye Three Roses*. Wow-wow-wow, what a woman! And when his personal feelings regarding Nanette were discussed, he described her as too playful, not serious enough. According to Barry Wielen, love was a serious business. And Nanette was not serious.

A different description was added by Frank Bogaard, her loving cousin? Bitterly he described her as a poisonous snake in the shape of an angel.

DeKok scratched the back of his neck. Who to believe? Which version was true? It just did not fit together. It was all too contradictory. An unknown, but undoubtedly highly talented painter had seen a completely different Nanette. Not a carefree person at all. Nor a poisonous snake, but a darling young woman, with a soft, sad look in her eyes, a somber nude.

Suddenly DeKok jumped off the desk.

"Come on," he said to Vledder, "we're going to do the rounds with the painting."

"Where to?"

Before DeKok could answer, the phone rang.

Vledder picked it up and listened.

He replaced the receiver after a few minutes. His face was pale as a ghost.

DeKok looked at him searchingly.

"What's the matter?" he asked.

Vledder swallowed with difficulty.

"At the garbage dump, near Canal F, they found the pieces of a young woman."

12

Canal F.

Just outside Amsterdam, past the Western Harbor are a series of canals. The canals form a grid. The Municipal Garbage Dump surrounds the canals which have been expressly dug for the purpose. A lot of garbage in Amsterdam is collected in barges. Even some of the garbage collected by trucks is dumped in barges, which all eventually find their way to Canal A, B, C, or whatever. These particular waterways are the only waterways in Holland without a name. Just a letter. It could have been a number. There the garbage is dumped, sorted, processed and eventually converted into various kinds of fertilizer, or relegated to landfills.

Vledder was forced to drive around the Harbor until he found the entrance to the dump. From there a barely discernable road led across the terrain. The road was mainly visible because there seemed to be less garbage on it, then in other places. It had started to rain again. The wipers of the old VW tried to keep up with it, but barely succeeded. The view through the windshield was vague and distorted.

Carefully, across a swaying pontoon bridge, they

reached the far side of Canal F. Steel plates indicated a path to a field. A wide, sad, stinking field, full of garbage.

Off to one side, close by, was a small town, a hole-in-the-wall. Rustic was the name of the town. Considering its proximity to the garbage dump, it could hardly have been named less appropriately. In the distance, behind a misty veil, Amsterdam could just be discerned between the rain storms. The steel plates ended between two immense mountains of garbage. It was the end of the road. Vledder stopped the car. Near a Caterpillar in the distance they noticed a group of men.

The two detectives got out of the car. Silently they approached the men. There were four; broad, strong types of the Amsterdam Municipal Sanitation Department. Their weather beaten, somber faces looked shiny in the rain, They moved out of the way. A dirty piece of canvas was on the ground, at their feet.

A slightly graying man, apparently the oldest of the group, looked up, turned to DeKok and asked:

"You're from Homicide?"

"Warmoes Street," admitted DeKok, nodding.

The man rubbed the rain from his face with the sleeve of his slicker.

"Just look," he said. His voice trembled.

He leaned over, took a corner of the canvass and lifted it carefully. Slowly a head became visible; a roughly severed girl's head.

* * *

DeKok felt the blood drain from his head. His stomach rebelled. He swallowed quickly and took a deep breath to suppress the inclination to vomit. He heard Vledder panting

130

next to him. DeKok pulled the collar of his raincoat closer around his neck, trying to close the gap between the coat and his hat. It was a ridiculous gesture. He just needed time to get over his revulsion. Any confrontation with death confused him, slowed his thinking. Despite his years and years of experience and his many encounters with violent death, he had never been able to get used to it. Usually he was able to hide his emotions behind an expressionless, cold facade. This time, too, he needed to force himself to take a closer look at the head. He squatted down next to the man and lifted the canvass slightly higher.

The face was waxen. The almost transparent skin was covered with dirt and crusts of coagulated blood. The long, blonde hair was flattened by the rain and stuck around the neck, mercifully hiding some of the horror that was visible there. The head had been severed just above the torso. DeKok looked at the half-open eyes. Carefully he lifted the eyelids, one by one. The irises were cornflower blue. He looked around. Within his grasp he found a few pieces of a broken clothes hanger. He picked up a piece and used it to lift the upper lip slightly and pressed down on the lower lip. The mouth was partially open. Two rows of beautifully maintained, straight, pearly white teeth became visible. There seemed to be no fillings in the molars.

DeKok threw the piece of cloth hanger from him and let the description of the disappeared girl pass in review. There was no doubt, none whatsoever. The severed head was that of Nanette Bogaard.

DeKok pressed his lips together. His fears had come true. Nanette had been killed, horribly murdered. The murderer had even taken the time and the trouble to sever the head.

He looked at the man who had squatted down, next to him.

"Is this all you found?"

The man shook his head.

"Over there," he said somberly, "is the rest."

Carefully, with a tender gesture that was almost devout, he covered the girl's head with the scrap of canvass. Then he rose and walked away. DeKok, Vledder and the others followed him. Slowly they walked in single file. Silent. A silent procession in the rain, among mud, dirt, garbage and discarded household items. Their shoes sank in the mud as if they were crossing a swamp. The damp stink of decay permeated everything. A couple of crows sheltered under a rusty furnace. As the men passed, the birds flew away, screeching loudly. A large, yellow doll, missing one leg, stared at the sky and displayed a soulless smile.

Next to a few pieces of cardboard, in the shelter of the bulldozer, the older man halted. Patiently he waited for all of them to join him. They formed a circle. Then he removed the cardboard. The shock was slightly less, this time.

Apart from each other, but close, were the missing parts of the body: both arms, the long, slender legs, the petite torso. There was no clothing, neither on the legs, nor on the torso. The red nail polish on the toes contrasted sharply with the pale, waxen look of the limbs. In contrast to the head, there seemed to be less dirt and blood on the remaining body parts. Apparently they had been laying in the rain a little longer and had been washed by it.

DeKok bent over to take a closer look at the disfigurements. It seemed that somebody with a certain amount of anatomical knowledge, had been at work. It seemed almost professional. There was no question of a hasty, panicky butcher job. He had seen that too many times in the past. On the contrary, in order to remove the limbs from the torso, only the absolute minimum of cuts had been applied. Yes, concluded DeKok, that took more than a smattering of anatomical knowledge.

His glance drifted to the petite torso. As far as he could see, there were no other, outward indications of injury, or mutilation.

DeKok remained in a squatting position for some time. Subconsciously his thoughts went to the large doll they had just passed, the doll with the frozen smile and the single leg. Thrown out. Children had played with it. They had walked with it. Had dressed it, undressed it, cared for it. Until . . .

"My wife." he said suddenly, loudly, "still keeps the dolls from her childhood."

"What?" asked Vledder.

DeKok looked at him, confused, absent-mined. He rubbed his eyes with a tired gesture.

"Nothing, my boy, nothing," he answered, evading the question. "Nothing at all, at all."

He rose slowly and turned to the older man, apparently the foreman.

"Did you find all the pieces?"

"Yes."

"What's your name?"

"Claus . . . Claus Boer."

DeKok turned to Vledder and signalled him to take notes.

"What did you find first?"

The man from the Sanitation Department did not answer at once. He took the large pieces of cardboard and carefully covered the body parts.

"First I found a leg."

"And then?"

The man turned and gestured around.

"Look, mister, when the garbage is dumped from the trucks, or lifted from the barges, with the crane, there, you get heaps, big heaps. Big heaps of garbage. The first task is to smooth it out. I use the bulldozer and I smooth it out, equalize it, so to speak. Of course, there's all kinds of stuff in the garbage. You find the craziest things, sometimes. Usually you don't even notice it. It's all just garbage, you see. But this morning, suddenly, I saw a leg stick out of the dirt. At first I thought it was the leg of a mannequin, you know, a store dummy. That happens often, sometimes. But it looked so real, you know, too real to be the leg of a dummy. Well, I stopped the machine and took a closer look. It was really a leg, you know, a real leg, I mean."

"What did you do then?"

"I wanted to call the police right-a-way. But we're sorta isolated here, you know. There's no phone nearby. It's a good twenty minute walk, near the main gate. So, I decided to wait for somebody. There are no barges due today, but the trucks do come in all the time."

The man wiped the rain from his face, then continued.

"Anyway, I lifted the leg from the garbage and put it aside. A little later I found an arm. I really started to look then, you know. It wasn't too difficult. It took me less than fifteen minutes to find all the pieces."

"The head, too?"

"No, I found that later, you know. But these other were here already, then, I mean, and I had already asked somebody to call you."

DeKok nodded.

"Did you find the pieces far apart?"

"No, I mean, no, they were all more or less close together, you know. I figure something like, . . . eh, within a thirty, forty five foot area. Not farther, anyway. You know, I think it all came from the same truck."

"When?"

"Yesterday . . . yes, yesterday. In the afternoon, I think. You see, we work alternately, you know, I mean, what is dumped today, is equalized tomorrow, you know. And what was dumped yesterday, is equalized today, you see. So I was working here, so it was dumped yesterday. And here I found it."

Slowly DeKok glanced around the enormous mountains of garbage.

"Mr. Boer," he said after a while, "do you have any idea where this particular garbage could have originated?"

"You mean . . . eh, the garbage with the . . . eh, parts?"

"Yes."

"Well, that's a bit difficult, mister. In any case, it's from West. Yes, Amsterdam West. But where exactly, I don't know, it could be any of a lot of neighborhoods, you know, take your pick, Ditch Canal, Mill Lake, Ox Village, Halfway, who knows. That's almost impossible to figure out exactly. If it had come by barge, it might have been easier. The crane driver usually knows where the barges come from, but that's usually the old part of town, you know. West all comes by truck."

DeKok smiled faintly.

"That's quite an area. Half Amsterdam lives in West.

The man made a helpless gesture.

"Yes, I understand," he said sympathetically. "Yes, I understand it's difficult for you. Yes, I know, I mean, it's important for you to know where the dirt came from. You need that information. Believe me, if I could help you, I would be only too glad to do so. But even if I knew exactly what truck had dumped that particular load of garbage, you still wouldn't get much farther, you know. I mean, the trucks we use today have a much larger load capacity, you know. They can cover a large area."

"All right, but is it possible to assume that the body parts you found, along with the garbage in which they were found, all came from the same truck?"

The Sanitation man nodded emphatically.

"Oh, yes, you can assume that."

"Thus I can rule out the possibility that the corpse, the pieces of the corpse, came to be here in any other way?"

"Absolutely."

"Excellent."

The closing of a car door made him look around. A special unit of the Municipal Medical Service had arrived. It was one of the units usually sent out in the case of drowning incidents. There must have been a mix-up in the dispatching office. The coroner's van would have been more appropriate. But perhaps there was a shortage of manpower, because the crew seemed to know what was wanted. The paramedics left the ambulance and came closer. Slowly they came closer. They carried a large, galvanized kettle between them.

"Vledder pointed at the body parts.

With impassive, bored faces they gathered the head, the arms, the legs and the torso and placed them in the kettle. There was not a sign of emotion, The sanitation workers looked pale.

"Please take it all directly to the pathology lab," said DeKok.

The older of the two paramedics nodded.

"You know the name of the victim, already?" he asked.

"Nanette ... Nanette Bogaard," DeKok swallowed a lump in his throat.

The paramedic took a note book and wrote it down.

"Do you claim ownership in the name of justice?" he asked formally.

"Yes, my name is DeKok, with ... eh, kay-oh-kay, Homicide, Warmoes Street."

The paramedic closed his notebook and placed it in the breast pocket of his uniform coat. Then he and his colleague lifted the kettle between them and walked back to the ambulance. Their free arms swung back and forth to equalize the load.

* * *

After the ambulance, with its grim load had disappeared, the gray man took DeKok by the sleeve.

"Did I hear you mention the name of the girl?" he asked.

"Yes ...?"

The man hesitated.

"Was it ... eh, was it a bad girl?"

DeKok looked at him searchingly.

The man grinned, a bit shamefaced and embarrassed.

"I ... eh, I have a daughter, just like that, you see. She ... eh, reminded me a bit of my daughter, you know. I mean, sometimes you don't know what to do, or think. You can't watch them night and day, you know." He shook his gray head and sighed. "No, not night and day. You can only hope for the best, you know."

DeKok placed a comforting hand on his shoulder.

"Just do that," he said encouragingly. "Hope for the best. Luckily there are only a few that really wind up on the garbage heap, literally, I mean."

He bent down. The large, yellow doll with the missing leg was at his feet.

He picked it up.

"May I have this?"

The sanitation man looked at him in surprise.

"But of course, go ahead."

"Thank you."

He turned and walked back to the police car. The doll swung from one hand.

Vledder followed.

13

Young Vledder floored the gas pedal of the old VW. He drove fast, wild, as one possessed. Leaning forward over the wheel, a determined look on his face, he forced the old car to the limits of its capabilities. The engine whined in protest.

DeKok looked at him from the passenger seat.

"What's the matter, boyo?" he yelled over the sound of the engine, "are you in a hurry?"

Vledder did not answer. Intense, staring down the road, he proceeded with undiminished speed. At the end of the long road, alongside the canal, he side-slipped onto the wet pavement of the main highway, barely missing a truck as it came from the opposite direction. As if there was no other traffic, Vledder routinely, almost casually, brought the skid under control.

DeKok shook his head and grinned.

"What are you trying to do?" he asked cynically, "are you trying to overtake death, or are you fleeing it? It doesn't matter, you know. No matter what, death always wins in the end."

"Funny . . .," spat Vledder. "Oh, real funny, I must say. Mister Detective makes jokes. Real funny jokes about death."

DeKok pushed his lower lip forward. He did not react in any other way. He had not meant to be funny. Not at all. It had been more a warning against speeding. He doubted if Vledder had taken it as a joke. He did not think so. It had been more like a blind lashing out at something, anything. He knew his pupil well enough, to have some idea of how he felt at this point. The horrible discovery at the dump had touched him; disturbed his equilibrium, so to speak. He had noticed that before. The boy took it too much to heart. Too sensitive. He had not learned, yet, how to disassociate his emotions and feelings from the unpleasant aspects of the job.

Near the city they encountered the usual grid-lock. They were able to proceed at no more than a snail's pace. DeKok did not mind at all. He slid comfortably down in his seat and inspected the doll he had picked up at the dump. Vledder looked at him from aside and grinned sarcastically.

"A young girl has been put to death in a most horrible way," he said. "So horrible, that the pieces had to be gathered from all over the place. And what do we find, occupies the brain of the great sleuth?" He snorted derisively. "The great sleuth asks the garbage man, oh so politely, if he can please have an old, dirty, broken doll."

He moved the car a few more feet and shook his head in desperation.

"Dammit, DeKok, there are more important things to be concerned about than an old doll with one leg."

"Such as . . .?"

Vledder gave him an angry look.

"Such as solving the murder," he said tersely.

DeKok sighed a deep sigh.

"You see," he said, resignedly, "that's exactly what occupies me at the moment."

* * *

Corporal Bykerk, who was acting as desk-sergeant, elevated his considerable bulk from the chair behind the desk as Vledder and DeKok entered the lobby of the old, renowned police station at Warmoes Street.

"What about the report from the dump?" he asked. "Can I cancel the APB for the Bogaard girl?"

Slowly DeKok nodded.

"Yes, you may. We don't have to find her anymore. We found her. In pieces. Murdered." He grimaced in Vledder's direction. "Now we only need the murderer," he concluded.

Corporal Bykerk grinned understanding.

"Is that all?" he asked.

"Ach," said DeKok, "that shouldn't take my partner too long."

Vledder looked angry. With a face like a thundercloud he turned and wanted to climb the stairs to the detective room. But Bykerk called him back.

"There's somebody waiting for you in three," he called. "I think he can tell you a thing or two about the Bogaard girl. He's been waiting more than an hour, already."

Vledder looked at him suspiciously.

"Who?"

Bykerk looked at his notes.

"One Ronald Staaten. I kept him for you, for the moment. He asked for Inspector DeKok and told me that he came in connection with the disappearance of Nanette Bogaard. That is, if your old mentor allows it . . . he's in interrogation three. At least you have something to start with."

DeKok nodded agreement.

"All right. Yes, a good idea. I have the feeling that friend Vledder would just love to ask him a few questions, penetrating questions, super intelligent questions. Isn't that so, my boy?"

Vledder growled something they could not understand.

Bykerk laughed out loud.

* * *

Ronald Staaten seemed very sure of himself. As Vledder and DeKok entered the interrogation room, he stood up, made a polite bow, and calmly reseated himself.

"My father," he spoke in an affected voice, "imparted to me the knowledge that the gentlemen of the police were vitally interested in my humble self." He made a small, artistic gesture with his hand and showed two rows of even, white teeth. "Well, as you perceive, here I am," he concluded.

DeKok nodded slowly.

"We can see that," he conceded, "yes, we can see that." He pointed in the direction of Vledder.

"My colleague will ask you a few questions. You must understand that this is just routine. But I strongly urge you not to take liberties with reality."

Staaten grinned.

"The truth and nothing but the truth."

He seemed to be amused by his witticism. He crossed his arms in front of his chest and presented a picture of self-satisfaction.

DeKok rubbed his hand over his face.

"Truth," he said with emphasis, "truth is never a subject for jokes, it is seldom funny."

Ronald shrugged his shoulders nonchalantly and Vledder pulled a chair closer.

"You still live at home, with your father?"

"Yes."

"Do you have any brothers, or sisters?"

"No."

As Vledder started the interrogation, DeKok took the opportunity to study Ronald Staaten at length. Ronald, he thought, had little in common with his father, the broker. There was no similarity, either in behavior, or appearance. Ronald was a slender young man with blond, shoulder length, wavy hair, green eyes and soft, almost weak facial features. Handsome in a repugnant, almost unmanly, way.

He portrayed an attitude of conscious challenge, almost provocation. Smiling, irritating, in a deep purple jacket with flowers and a light colored pair of slacks, he answered Vledder's questions.

"Do you get along with your father?"

"Do I have to answer that?"

"If you like."

"No."

"Why not?"

Ronald grinned, it was not a pleasant sight.

"What young man, my age, is able to co-exist with his father? We tolerate each other. That is probably the most positive statement I can make regarding our relationship."

"That was different, until recently?"

"What *do* you mean?"

"I understand from your father, that you grew closer together, after the death of your mother. He spoke of a good father-son relationship."

Ronald did not answer at once. He lowered his head somewhat. For the first time, some of his arrogant manner seemed to leave him.

143

"What could I do?" he asked after a while. "He was all that was left to me, all I had. I could hardly ask for consolation from the neighbors. Right? After all, he *is* my father."

Vledder hesitated a moment.

"That ... eh, that sounds bitter."

"Yes!" screamed young Staaten. "You're right! It sounds bitter. I know it. But do you know why my mother died? Well, do you? No, of course not. You don't know that. You don't know anything! Well, I'll tell you! I'll tell you about that clapped out Don Juan! My mother died of shame, of humiliation!"

"Humiliation?"

"Yes, humiliated by the hundreds of affairs of my father, with women of every age, kind, color, race, type, you name it."

"And your mother knew that?"

Ronald nodded emphatically.

"My father even had the unmitigated gall, the impudence, the insolence, I should say, to boast about his so-called conquests to others, in my mother's presence. Just think about that, if you will."

He shook his head several times.

"My mother ... my mother was a dear, soft, gentle woman. She never said anything, she never complained. She never openly objected to my father's behavior. She suffered in silence."

Vledder swallowed and pushed his chair back. Meanwhile he glanced quickly at DeKok, who was leaning against the wall, out of Ronald's line of sight. An encouraging nod from his mentor, convinced him that he should continue the interrogation in the same vein.

"You mother confided in you?"

144

"Yes."

"So that, what she knew of your father's adventures, you knew as well. You shared the knowledge?"

"Indeed, mother had no secrets from me."

"Did you ever discuss divorce with her?"

"Mother didn't want a divorce."

"Why not?"

"First, because of religious considerations. Mother was very devout. Also, she wanted to insure my inheritance."

Vledder tried to raise his eyebrows.

"Insure?" he asked.

"Yes, you understand, as long as the marriage between my parents wasn't dissolved, I remained the sole heir. Mother wanted to keep it that way. If she had ever decided on divorce, father would almost certainly have remarried and who knows how many legal offspring would have been the result of that."

Vledder grinned broadly.

"And too many cooks spoil the broth."

"A rather inelegant remark, to say the least." Ronald reacted sharply. "I would almost call it insulting," he concluded.

A slight blush moved quickly over Vledder's face. The sharp tone of young Staaten was not, however, able to break the rhythm of the interrogation.

"But, if I understand you correctly," he continued calmly, "then, when your mother passed away, you held your father responsible for her death. Is that right?"

"Yes."

"You believe that your father's behavior affected your mother's health?"

"Yes."

"Did you ever tell him that?"

145

Ronald sighed.

"No, I never told him. He never gave me the chance, it's as simple as that."

Momentarily confused, Vledder stared at him.

"That ... eh, I don't understand that."

Ronald sighed again. It seemed to come from the bottom of his heart.

"After mother died, I decided to tell him, in no uncertain terms, what I thought of him. It was about time that someone should tell him the truth. As long as mother was alive I kept silent for her sake."

"And?"

Young Staaten rubbed a hand through his long hair. He shrugged his shoulders and made a defeated gesture.

"When the time came," he said softly and sadly, "I could not do it. You see, to my utter amazement, he showed real sorrow. My mother's death touched him deeply. He was really devastated by it. Thereby he took all weapons from me. I had no longer any incentive, you understand? He locked himself in his room and would not come out, for days at a time. It was a sort of penance, I thought."

Vledder looked at him searchingly.

"What exactly do you mean by 'thought'?"

The young man snorted contemptuously.

"Within a year after her death, he was already running around with some young chick."

"Nanette?"

"Yes," he answered, absent mindedly. "Yes, Nanette Bogaard. One night they both came to see me. Hand in hand ... and father, revolting, ... announced with a trembling voice, that they had come to an agreement and would marry soon."

Vledder stood up.

"And thus," he announced primly, "we arrive at the beginning of the drama. The drama of Nanette, or the struggle for the fatted calf."

14

Young Ronald reacted angrily. He pulled his lips together until they formed a thin, narrow line. His handsome young face showed hostility.

"What fatted calf?"

With his head slightly cocked, Vledder looked at him for some time.

"Come, come, Mr. Staaten," he said finally, friendly with infinite patience evident in his very words, "you know very well what I'm talking about ... the rather extensive fortune of your father."

"What does that have to do with it?"

"Everything! You couldn't have made it clearer. You're the sole heir. It was the express wish of your mother that this should remain so. Isn't that right? She was willing to suffer the shame and humiliation inflicted by your father. Just to preserve that. It is very understandable that you, as her son, want to make sure that your mother's wishes are honored, that they are abided by. In other words: you'll make sure that you remain the sole heir."

A tic developed on Staaten's left cheek.

"You ... eh," he said carefully, "you're insinuating ..."

"What?"

Staaten turned his head away from Vledder. He swallowed several times. His adam's apple bobbed up and down.

"You're insinuating that I have something to do with Nanette's disappearance."

Vledder sniffed.

"To put it mildly," he said, "you have an impressive motive for murder."

With a shock the young man sat up straight.

"Murder?"

"Exactly. Murder. And you could save yourself and us a lot of trouble if you were to tell us, right now, and without unnecessary evasions, when and where you killed Nanette Bogaard."

Staaten's eyes grew large and afraid. He looked at Vledder in surprise. All he saw was an unemotional, even face.

"Me . . .?" he whispered.

Vledder nodded silently.

Staaten could not ignore the statement. There was no way out. Strangely, nervously, like an idiot, he started to grin. All color had drained from his handsome face. Scared, he looked around him. With a silent appeal in his eyes he looked from Vledder to DeKok and back again. His eyes mirrored an attitude of doglike devotion.

"M-me . . .?" he stuttered, finally. "M-me . . . N-nanette. That's . . . eh, t-that's crazy! It is . . . eh, it's . . . You cannot mean it! N-no, you don't mean it." He kept shaking his head. "NO!" he screamed suddenly, "not me . . . not me . . ."

Vledder stood up. The denial did not affect him. On the contrary. He felt that Ronald Staaten was ready to confess. He judged that the broker's son had very little fight, very little resistance left. He only had to, he thought, he only had

150

to persevere. Until now he had built the interrogation neatly, step by step. According to the book. After establishing the motive, he had made an outright accusation. Just a matter of crossing the tees and dotting the eyes and the Nanette case was solved. It would be his first great triumph!

From his standing position he looked down at the scared young man on the chair. The deep purple jacket with flowers was no longer a challenge, a provocation. It was now just ridiculous.

"At first," he began slowly, "I didn't understand why you took Nanette's painting and sold it. I couldn't explain it. At first, it seemed so senseless."

He sighed demonstratively.

"But now I understand. It is as clear as day. The painting had to go ... away from the house. You couldn't stand to see it anymore. The beautiful, perfect body on the canvass was a constant reminder to you of her death, the terrible, disgusting disfigurement you inflicted ..."

Vledder had started to speak louder and faster as he progressed, building up to a climax in his recapitulation. His last words echoed against the bare, plaster walls of the small room. Then there was silence. Ronald Staaten looked stricken. He looked as if he had not understood a word. Senseless, unaware of his surroundings he stared in front of him. His mouth was half open.

Vledder became angry, irritated. The blood rushed to his head, pulsated at his temples. Accusingly he stretched his hand out to young Staaten. It was a theatrical gesture.

"You ...," he yelled, "you killed her! You! Nanette was in your way. You saw your inheritance threatened. You didn't want your father to marry again! You suddenly realized how vital, how virile he still was." Vledder imitated Ronald's voice mockingly: *"And who knows how many legal*

151

offspring would have been the result of that. Those are your own words."

Staaten did not react. He remained in a nebulous cloud of apathy. A cloud that seemed to protect him, insulate him from the world around him.

Angrily Vledder shook his head. He felt himself loosing his grip on the young man. His words did not have the desired result. They missed their mark. He became more angry thinking about it. He had felt himself so close to the solution, so close to his triumph; and now it was being washed away, like footsteps on the beach.

In a sudden fit of temper, he took Staaten by the lapels of his jacket and lifted him from his chair. His anger seemed to make him stronger. The silk-like fabric strained in his grip.

"Why," he hissed, "why did you sell the painting? Why?" He shook Staaten the way a dog shakes a rat. "Dammit, you bastard, open your mouth, why did you sell the painting? Answer me!"

The young man remained silent.

Vledder changed his tone. His eyes narrowed to slits.

"I'll answer it for you," he said softly, threateningly. "It was fear, yes, pure fear. That's what it was. You were afraid of the painting, the nude, the constant reminder, the accusation on the wall of your living room."

It seemed as if Ronald suddenly woke up, as if he came out of a coma. He looked Vledder in the eyes. His gaze was clear and steady. Softly, almost toneless, he said:

"It wasn't fear. No, it wasn't fear."

The denial irritated Vledder even more. His eyes spat fire. In a sudden explosion of near hysterical strength, he pressed Staaten against the wall of the interrogation room.

The chair was kicked out of the way and fell noisily in a corner of the room.

"It was fear," he screamed at the top of his voice. "You're lying, it *was* fear. Tell me ... tell me ... tell me ...!"

Vledder kept repeating himself. He was obviously beside himself. He was losing control. His voice broke.

DeKok saw the danger.

"Vledder!"

It sounded stern, there was condemnation in the voice.

"Let go of him and get out."

Vledder did not respond at once. It took a few seconds before DeKok's words penetrated. He closed his eyes tightly, shook his head, as if to clear it. The red mist of rage that had taken control of him, dissipated slowly. He let go of the young man. For a moment, still, he looked at his victim. Then he murmured: "sorry, really sorry" and, head down, he left the room.

DeKok watched him go. He knew so well how his pupil felt at this moment. Miserable. He remembered that from his early days, when he was young, like Vledder, and was faced with an inevitable defeat. It was almost impossible to accept. But those days were gone. The years had made him more experienced, but above all, the years had made him wiser.

Sighing, he picked up the fallen chair.

"Please sit down," he said in his friendliest tone of voice. "Are you all right? Did he hurt you?"

Staaten smiled faintly.

"It wasn't all that bad."

DeKok made an apologetic gesture.

"My colleague is ... eh, rather short-tempered. A bit over zealous, at times. Please don't hold that against him. Although his methods can be a bit unusual, at times, he's, after all, fighting for the truth. He's fighting the good fight, I mean, his motives are pure." His faced creased into a friendly smile, then he asked: "Don't you agree?"

Young Staaten managed a sad grin.

"Pure ..." he laughed mockingly, "what a choice of words. Your colleague wanted to force a confession out of me. Perhaps you consider that fighting the good fight, maybe you think that is *pure*, but I regret to inform you, that I do not share your opinion. His methods are contemptible."

He sank down in the chair, crossed his legs and rubbed both hands through his hair. Apparently he had recovered from Vledder's attack. His face had regained some color. He gestured in DeKok's direction.

"How can I possibly confess to something I haven't done? That's too crazy, don't you agree? Nanette is dead, that much I understood from your colleague's words. She's been killed, murdered. Well, that's sad, but I haven't done it. If you want to hold me responsible for her death, than that is strictly your own affair. But you'd better be able to prove it. So far, all I have heard, have been unsubstantiated accusations."

"I think," said the gray sleuth calmly, "that my colleague has made a rather clear and concise explanation of your motives."

"Motives, Shmotives," said Ronald defiantly. "Just because I may have a motive to kill someone, doesn't prove that I have. You should know that, better than anybody."

DeKok rubbed his hands over his craggy face. Staaten was right. There was no proof. Just motive was not enough for a trial. With just motives, the Judge-Advocate would not even think about prosecuting.

He closed his eyes momentarily. He felt tired, drained, exhausted. His feet started to hurt. That was always a bad sign. It always happened. When a case was not progressing, when he seemed to get farther and farther away from the solution, his feet would hurt. Sighing deeply, he slid further down in his chair and placed his feet on the table. With a painful grimace on his face he looked at young Staaten. He did not like the arrogant tone of the young man. The way in which he spoke about Nanette was cold, emotionless, without a grain of compassion for the victim. The death of the girl had not upset him in the least.

Again DeKok looked at the handsome, somewhat weak face. He saw continued, alert suspicion.

"You didn't kill Nanette?"

"No, I did *not* kill Nanette."

"You are not responsible for her death?"

"It has nothing to do with me."

Slowly DeKok nodded.

"Excellent," he said resignedly, "really excellent. I like to meet innocent people." It sounded solemn. He made a tired gesture. "Thus, you can answer my questions frankly. You can be truthful. There's no reason to hold anything back."

Ronald looked suspiciously at the old detective. He saw a tired man with the friendly face of a good natured boxer.

"Yes," he answered. He did not sound convinced. Then he added: "Yes, I suppose I can."

"Then I would like to repeat my partner's question: why did you sell Nanette's painting?"

Young Staaten's eyes narrowed. Again, obviously, the question shocked him. It did not escape DeKok. He watched a shudder go through the boy's body. Ronald became white around the nose. He did not answer.

155

DeKok took his legs off the table. He could not feel his feet anymore. The drained, disabling feeling had disappeared. His gaze rested on the young man.

"Well?" he pressed.

Staaten swallowed.

"The painting irritated me."

"Why?"

Ronald lowered his head. He seemed to wrestle with an answer. His nervous, searching fingers moved toward his dry lips.

"Because . . . eh, because of the setting."

"The setting?"

Suddenly Staaten jumped out of chair.

"Yes," he screamed, "the setting!"

He had lost control, all his arrogance, his self assurance was gone. His face was red and distorted. His lower lip trembled. Tears appeared in his eyes.

"The bastard," he exclaimed intensely, "t-the d-dirty, sneaky, f-filthy fiend." The words tumbled out. "He made her pose on the sofa. Naked, you understand, she had to sit naked on my mother's sofa. The sofa on which she used to rest, especially when she became ill. And he posed that naked slut on it. Even after her death, he had to humiliate her."

DeKok looked at him, incredulity on his face.

"Did he do that on purpose?"

Ronald nodded emphatically.

"Yes, just to pester me. To besmirch the memory of my mother, to make it cheap, tawdry." He ground his teeth. A hint of insanity was visible in the hard, green eyes. "I would have killed her," he hissed threateningly. "Oh, yes, you can be sure of that, I would have murdered her. Nanette was

156

never going to take my mother's place. Never!" His voice rose in pitch and he screamed: "Never! Never! Never!"

15

Ronald Staaten sobbed in sorrow and regret. In the small interrogation room, the noise seemed louder than it was. His head was resting on his arms, hiding his face. Long, deep sobs racked his body. Sometimes he shrieked a long wail.

DeKok stood and watched him. Without emotion. From his height he looked down at the shaking back of the young man in the deep purple jacket and he wondered if Ronald was really capable of murder, in thought, or in deed.

It was a hypothetical question. That much DeKok knew. He had seen many, many murderers during his long and varied career. All kind of killers. From cool, cold stranglers to emotional, hyper nervous shootists. He had never been able to find anything in common between them.

He had known men who killed somebody for a few bucks; just like that, without thought and without pity. He had known people who had been forced to kill, in self-defense, or for some other compelling reason, judicially guiltless, they always felt guilty and were constantly tortured by what they had done. Wild lions would turn out to be meek sheep and meek sheep could turn into ruthless killers. One never knew.

Slowly, over the years, he had come to the conclusion that anybody, no matter who, was capable of murder. It was no more than a game of chance, a game of chance consisting of facts, circumstances and emotions. If fate had stacked the deck in such a way that the required facts, circumstances and emotions coincided with the opportunity, murder could be the result. It did not matter who the players were. It was only a matter of degree.

DeKok pressed his lips together. What were the murder factors for Ronald Staaten? Thoughtfully he let them pass in review.

Only son of wealthy parents, the early death of the mother, who had practically been his sole anchor, the somewhat inflated vitality of the father who wanted to remarry at an advanced age, the hatred toward the father, the youth of Nanette, the nude on the sofa, the still very strong emotional bond with the mother. DeKok rubbed his face. It was all there.

He placed his hand on the head of the sobbing young man.

"Come," he said, compelling, but in a fatherly tone, "let's talk about it some more, together. Earnestly, man to man. Murder is worth discussing."

Slowly Staaten lifted his head.

DeKok looked in the teary face. Strangely enough, he felt no pity, no compassion. The sorrow, the regret, of the young man left him untouched. He did not care for crying men. They irked him. He took a clean handkerchief from his pocket and tossed it at Ronald.

"Here," he said gruffly, "clean your face."

He watched while the younger man wiped the tears from his eyes. Then he left the interrogation room and returned, a few minutes later, with two steaming mugs of coffee. He placed one mug in front of Staaten and started to slurp comfortably himself. Slowly the young man brought himself under control. He became calmer. DeKok noticed.

"But what I don't understand," he said, "is why you didn't protest against the use of the sofa, *before* the painting was done."

Carefully Staaten sipped from his coffee.

"I did not know."

"Didn't know what?"

"I had no idea what kind of painting it was going to be. One day Pierre Popko came to get the sofa . . ."

"Who's Pierre Popko?" interrupted DeKok.

"The painter, the one who made the painting."

"Right, and thus . . .?"

"I said: 'Pierre, what do you want with mother's sofa?' and he told me it was for a painting, commissioned by my father. He did not tell me any more and I did not ask. You see, I did not know that Pierre planned to use the sofa as a seat for Nanette, that he would pose Nanette, naked, on the sofa."

"Did you know Nanette at that time?"

"Yes, I did. She had come to our house several times, by then. It was about a month after Pierre introduced us to her."

Surprised DeKok stared at him.

"Nanette was introduced to you, and your father, by Pierre Popko?"

Ronald nodded.

"In addition to his other activities," he said with a down-turned mouth, "father is also a sort of *maecenas*, a guardian angel, a patron of art and artists. Pierre Popko is one of his protegees. He gave him commissions, introduced him to his friends. Pierre used to visit us often. Also when

161

mother was still alive. Well ... one evening he was accompanied by Nanette."

"I thought," said DeKok, "that your father had made the acquaintance of the lady through his interest in ... eh, botanical subjects."

"Oh, you must have seen the rose in his lapel."

"Yes, that's what I mean."

The young man shook his head.

"You don't know father," he said, grinning broadly. "If he met a young woman today who cannot stand alcohol, then father will be on the wagon before the day is out. I just mean to say, father did not start the flower routine, until after he discovered that Nanette worked in a flower shop."

DeKok laughed.

"Yet, Nanette seemed to have made an impression on him. His marriage plans seemed in earnest."

"Father was very much taken with her, charmed is the word, I think. Certainly. He lived in a sort of dream. The fact that a beautiful young girl was interested in him, flattered his vanity, if nothing else. What would you expect?"

Young Staaten paused briefly, shook his head and sighed deeply.

"Pierre Popko encouraged it strongly. He showed him sketches he had made of Nanette. He would praise her. He called her a goddess, a reincarnated Venus, perfection personified. And father, the old goat, listened with glowing ears and bated breath."

"What kind of sketches were they?"

"Just sketches. Charcoal sketches. Nude studies, of course. Nude studies of Nanette."

"Were they good? I mean, did you like them? Were they done well, realistic?"

162

"They were so realistic," he grinned, "that father bought them all. Once he decided that he would marry her, he didn't want Pierre to make any more sketches of her. He did not want anybody else to have her pictures. He also prohibited Nanette to pose again."

"Did Nanette obey him?"

"I don't know. I didn't check up on her."

DeKok looked up with sudden interest. He had detected a certain intonation in the young man's voice. A certain emphasis.

"You didn't," he asked sharply, "who did?"

Staaten did not answer at once. He moved restlessly in his chair. Apparently he was a bit embarrassed by the question.

"Well," pressed DeKok, "who did check up on her?"

Ronald swallowed.

"Father, he . . . eh, he did not trust Pierre."

* * *

DeKok was sitting behind his desk and stared somberly at nothing at all. He was stuck. He was not getting any closer. It was too slow. There was no movement in the case, no progress. So far, all the people he had contacted in connection with Nanette, were difficult, lied, or told half truths. For example, Kristel must have known something about the intended marriage of Nanette. Why had she not mentioned it? And Barry Wielen? Without a doubt he had been the mysterious tipster that had led them to the painting. But how did he know about the painting? What exactly *did* he know? Undoubtedly more than he was telling.

Thinking hard, DeKok rubbed his chin. The sheet on which he had been doodling was still on his desk. The line he had written was still there: HOW OR WHY OR THROUGH WHOM DID NANETTE DISAPPEAR? He had only written that yesterday. Really, he should not be too dissatisfied with the results so far. Now, only a day later, he was already able to answer part of the question. Nanette disappeared because she had been killed, murdered by someone who, for one reason or another, had found it necessary to mutilate the corpse in a most abhorrent manner. Especially the last part seemed important to him. Why the disfigurement? What had been the purpose?

Vledder entered the detective room. He seemed hurried and excited. He hung his wet raincoat from a peg and pushed a chair closer to DeKok's desk. His face beamed.

"Did you know," he whispered, "that Nanette used to be a nurse?"

DeKok nodded slowly.

"I suspected as much," he said resignedly.

"Well, it's true. When I went to Aalsmeer to ask some questions, that's one of the things I heard. I suddenly remembered it, while you were talking to Ronald Staaten. Before Nanette and Kristel started their flower shop, Nanette was a nurse, or a student nurse. I hadn't told you yet. You see, at first I didn't think it too important."

Laughing, DeKok looked at him.

"And then you thought about Brother Laurens?"

"Exactly," he exclaimed enthusiastically, "Brother Laurens! You understand, the morphine. Of course, Nanette must have gotten to know Brother Laurens during her stint as a nurse. That's reasonable. During that time she got a hold over him, somehow and then she forced him to deliver the drugs to her. That's the way it went, don't you think?"

"It's possible," answered the gray sleuth carefully.

Vledder's face became disappointed.

"Now what!?" he asked, irked. "It *is* possible. That's the way it was. Absolutely. It's simply obvious. As soon as we catch Brother Laurens, you'll see I'm right."

"And how do you propose to 'catch' Brother Laurens?"

Vledder made a nonchalant gesture, suggesting that these were mere details.

"Simple. If we trace Nanette's history, her career as a nurse, then we can't help but find Brother Laurens. I've been working on it already."

"So . . ."

"Yes, I just came from *Ye Three Roses*. Kristel van Daalen even had a picture of Nanette in nurse's uniform"

Shocked, DeKok looked up.

"Did you tell her?"

"What?"

"That we found Nanette."

"No . . . eh, I . . . eh, no, I told her nothing."

"Didn't she ask?"

"No, she didn't ask anything. She did tell me all about how Nanette had become a nurse, how she was interested in surgery . . . Kristel was really nice. Friendly. I was asked to convey her regards to you."

DeKok snorted.

"How charming."

Startled, Vledder looked at him, surprised by the tone of voice.

"Is . . . eh, is something the matter?"

DeKok bent his head slightly and used a thumb and index finger to rub along the side of his nose, toward the corners of his eyes.

165

"No, nothing," he said wearily. "Nothing. It's all right, already. Go ahead. Follow the trail of Nanette's nursing career. Perhaps it *will* lead to Brother Laurens."

He raised a cautioning finger.

"But no further. I mean, as long as we know where to find him, that'll be enough for the moment."

"No arrest?"

"Not yet, my boy, not yet. We still do not know enough about his activities. He's still a rather vague figure. Even the suspicion that he should have anything to do with Nanette and drugs, is only the result of supposition, not fact. Just think about that."

He paused and chewed thoughtfully on his lower lip.

"Just one thing," he said pensively, "interests me no end . . ."

"What?"

DeKok stared in front of him.

"Did Brother Laurens share Nanette's interest in surgery?"

The phone rang at that moment.

Vledder picked it up and listened.

"It's for you," he said and handed the receiver to DeKok.

"Yes, DeKok here."

"You let him go," said a familiar voice he recognized instantly.

"*You let him go!*"

There was despair and disbelief in the voice.

"DeKok, why? You had him, you had him in your hands, all you had to do was turn the key and lock him up."

"Lock who up?"

"Young Staaten."

"Well, and?"

166

"He's the murderer. He's the one who killed Nanette Bogaard!"

DeKok sat up straight.

"What!?"

"Yes, Ronald. On the day Nanette disappeared he had a date with her."

16

Furious, DeKok threw the receiver back on the phone.

"Who was it?" asked Vledder.

"Wielen," he answered tersely. "He came right out and stated that Nanette has been killed by young Staaten."

"What?"

"Yes, he said that he simply couldn't understand why we didn't keep him, why we let him go. According to Wielen, the young man had a date with Nanette on the day she disappeared. He's supposed to have killed her at that time."

Vledder frowned.

"How does he know about the date?"

Morosely, DeKok shrugged his shoulders.

"He knows so many things, our reporter, for instance about the painting at the Mirror's Canal. You'll remember *he* was the one who called us."

Vledder nodded agreement.

"Yes, and he was also the man who wanted to buy the somber nude, regardless of price."

"Exactly. Wielen is up to his neck in this case. And his interest is more than just professional curiosity. Much more. He's personally involved. He loved Nanette and love can be the cause of the strangest situations."

DeKok narrowed his eyes to mere slits.

"But what I find so strange, what I don't understand at all, at all, is how does Wielen know that Nanette has been *murdered*! You see, our find at the Municipal Dump has not yet been made public. Apart from the men there, and the paramedics, only the police know about the mutilated corpse."

Vledder looked at him with admiration.

"You're right. Wielen *does* know more than he should know. That's suspicious, very suspicious, don't you agree?"

DeKok nodded. He stood up and shuffled over to the peg above the puddle created by his dripping raincoat. He was revitalized. He started to enjoy his job again. There was progress in the case. He placed his old, ridiculous little hat firmly on top of his head and struggled into the still wet, leaky raincoat.

"Come on, my boy," he said jovially. "it's about time that we present friend Wielen with an very apt proverb."

"A proverb?" Vledder looked dumbfounded.

"Never heard of it?" asked the old detective, grinning. "Very well known, I assure you: 'the more you know, the more you have to answer for'." He moved toward the door.

Vledder's entire face was transformed by a wide grin.

* * *

Barry Wielen looked tired, exhausted, as if he had not slept for days on end. His gray eyes looked dull. His face was gray. Even his remarkable mustache drooped. With a melancholy gaze he stared at DeKok.

"I expected you," he said with a deep sigh, "more or less. To tell you the truth, that's why I stayed home."

"Uncommonly accommodating."

170

"Nothing to do with being accommodating," answered Wielen, shaking his head, "you owe me an explanation. That's what I'm waiting for. Why did you let Ronald Staaten go? Why didn't you arrest him?"

His voice sounded demanding. He seemed to mean what he said.

"You let him go," he continued, "without checking the facts, or the background. That's unforgivable. You let a murderer go free."

DeKok looked at him without emotion and did not react.

Wielen became excited. He raised his voice.

"If you don't arrest Nanette's killer within twenty four hours," he yelled, "I'll write a piece about you that will destroy your reputation forever. You hear me? You'll be ruined as a policeman. Forever! I won't leave a piece of you intact!"

Not in the least impressed, DeKok waited patiently until he was through. Then he rose slowly from the easy chair in which he had lowered himself not too long ago. His broad face looked serious. Carefully he extended a hand toward the reporter.

"My sincere condolences," he said soberly, formally, "I sympathize with your loss. The loss of Nanette Bogaard, the young woman who was the object of your love and devotion. The news of her death must have been a shock for you."

Wielen hesitated momentarily. He searched DeKok's face. He was trying to find a trace of mockery, of insincerity. He could not find it. Then he took the extended hand.

"Thank you," he said hoarsely.

"I would have liked to soften the shock for you. For instance, I would have preferred to be the one to bring you the news, but, from your phone call, I understand that you had already heard?"

It was both a statement and a question. Wielen nodded.

"Somebody called me."

"Who?"

The reporter made a vague gesture.

"I, . . . eh, I've acquaintances with the police. They keep me informed of interesting cases, developments."

The sad, somewhat mild expression on DeKok's face changed. It turned cold, it became an icy mask.

"Interesting cases, developments," he said, biting, sardonic. "Yes, such as the discovery of the dismembered corpse of a young woman, a lively young woman. A woman you knew, a woman you loved, a woman you cared for. Interesting, no doubt, especially for the press."

Wielen covered his face with his hands.

"Stop it!" he screamed, "stop it!"

DeKok snorted. His nostrils trembled.

"Nanette Bogaard . . . What did you call her again? . . . Oh, yes, the wild daisy from *Ye Three Roses*! . . . A treasure! Wow-wow-wow, what a woman. *And you had not seen her for at least two weeks!*" his voice dripped with sarcasm.

Wielen groaned. DeKok's words hurt him. They hurt him to the quick, to the deepest, most hidden part of his soul. He dropped into a low chair. With difficulty he managed to swallow his tears.

DeKok, too, sat down again. His anger had gone. He had hurt the young man on purpose. It had been premeditated. He had to break through the resistance. Comfortably he stretched his legs and looked around the room. A small porcelain vase, filled with wild flowers, stood on a bookshelf. The stems were already wilting.

"If," he said calmly, "you had been a bit more forthright with me, from the beginning, if you had been more honest, more open, than I wouldn't have needed another twenty four hours to arrest the killer. Perhaps I'd *know*, even now, who killed her."

His tone changed, it became sharper.

"All right," he continued, "you've been playing your cat-and-mouse game long enough. The time has come to lay the facts on the table." He leaned forward, threatening, intimidating. "And believe me," he said harshly, "if you try to hide the smallest detail, I won't leave a piece of *you* intact."

A hint of a smile was briefly visible underneath the heavy mustache of the reporter.

"You're right," he sighed. "At first I didn't think it was all that serious. I was thinking in terms of an exclusive for the paper, I was more concerned about my scoop, than about Nanette. You see, Nanette was, as I saw it, not at all the type of girl to get into trouble. She was too independent, too . . . eh, too detached. You understand, she was . . . mercurial. Just when you thought you had her pinned down, she would slip through your fingers. Slippery, untouchable, not at all the type to fall into seven canals at the same time, as we say in Holland."

"You only need one canal to drown," observed DeKok.

Wielen nodded slowly.

"Indeed," he agreed somberly, "That's obvious, after the fact. She wasn't as slippery as I thought. Somebody got a hold of her . . ."

They remained silent for a long time. DeKok was the first to break the silence.

"But your attitude in this whole affair is not at all clear. Not easily explained. For instance, why did you tell us about

173

her visit to the Red Light District, something that happened two weeks ago, while you kept quiet about the date she had with Ronald Staaten, on the day of her disappearance? It seems to me that you were deliberately trying to mislead the police."

"I did, you're right. You see, I loved Nanette. I knew about her secret visits to the District. It intrigued me. Obviously! But I've never been able to find a reasonable explanation for it."

DeKok grinned. His craggy face was transformed into a picture of boyish mischief.

"And thus you thought: this is an excellent opportunity. If I give the police a hint, then they'll solve the problem for me. Isn't that right?"

Wielen sighed, a mixture of regret and a guilty conscience.

"It could have been a lead," he said apologetically, "it could have had something to do with her disappearance."

"But you didn't believe that yourself?" challenged DeKok.

"No, not really. I didn't really believe that. I looked at it more as a joke, one of Nanette's little tricks to get rid of Old Mealymouth."

DeKok's eyebrows were poised for one of their remarkable performances.

"Old Mealymouth?"

"That's what she called Staaten, the stockbroker."

"Why?"

"He pursued her, day and night, with proposals of marriage. Staaten is a rich man. He kept repeating what he could offer her, in addition to his own sweet, charming self."

"And?"

Irritated, Wielen looked up.

"What do you mean . . . and?" he asked.

"What was Nanette's response?"

"Of course, she didn't want anything to do with the old goat. After all, he was almost three times as old as she. As he persisted, at wit's end, she finally made an appointment with Ronald. She wanted to ask *him* to ask his father to stop pestering her. You understand?"

"Yes, I understand," nodded DeKok, "and she made the date for the day she disappeared?"

"Exactly. I saw her that day in *Ye Three Roses* and I bought, as you noticed so astutely, the bouquet of wild flowers. That's when she told me about her meeting with Ronald."

"Therefore you concluded that Ronald killed Nanette?"

"Yes, that's obvious. After that, nobody has seen Nanette alive. He must have killed her."

"And what about the motive?"

Wielen shrugged his shoulders.

"Perhaps," he said, hesitatingly, "perhaps, he was afraid that his father would marry Nanette anyway."

"Against her will?"

A painful expression came over the reporter's face.

"You never know," he admitted reluctantly. "Money . . . money is a powerful inducement, after all."

DeKok smiled.

"Your faith in her left room for doubt?"

Wielen made a sad gesture.

"Nanette was, after all, a woman." He seemed to think it explained everything.

DeKok took a closer look at the young man. In his heart he felt a mild affection, a form of sympathy. It was if he

175

discovered something of himself in the journalist, a similar way of looking at things. After a while he said:

"Tell me about the painting." His voice was friendly.

"The nude?"

"Indeed, the nude on the red sofa," he nodded.

"Nanette," Wielen answered lazily, "used to work as a model. It was a way for her to earn some extra pocket money. I was against it." He made a helpless gesture. "But what could I do about it? After all, I had no authority over her, and as far as influence is concerned . . . she was the type who simply could not be told."

He sighed deeply.

"She did what she wanted," he continued. "Pierre Popko, her favorite painter, if that's the word, had painted her nude, on a sofa. It was an extremely good painting, striking. I saw it, just after it was finished."

"Where?"

"In his studio, on Prince's Island. I used to pick Nanette up, from time to time, after she had been modelling."

"And?"

"I think that Nanette raised the subject with old Staaten, somehow. In any case, he bought the painting from Popko and gave it pride of place in his living room. I was furious when I heard about it. What the hell did that old goat want with a nude Nanette on his wall? One day, in a rash mood, I went to Staaten. I'd had a few drinks and I bluntly made him an offer for the painting. I didn't have all that much, but believe me, I would have spent every last cent to get that painting."

A faint smile was visible behind the moustache.

"Staaten looked at me as if I came from another planet. When he finally realized what I wanted, he laughed in my face. Church mouse, he called me, poor, destitute scribbler

". . . And then he showed me all his paintings. I wanted to punch him on his fat, rich face, but I missed. I think I must have been drinking more than I thought."

He paused again.

"Last night, rather late," he continued, "I was hanging around in the neighborhood of the Emperor's Canal."

"Near the Staaten residence?"

"Yes, you had been here earlier that day and told me that Nanette had disappeared and that Kristel had asked for her to be found. I knew that she, Nanette, that is, had a date with Ronald for the night before and I was hoping to catch a glimpse of her, to discover her whereabouts, so to speak. It would have made a nice article for the paper: Reporter finds missing girl."

"But there was no article," grinned DeKok.

"No," he sighed, again. "No, it didn't come to an article. I didn't see Nanette. All I saw was old Staaten, coming home around eleven thirty. That was all. At last I gave up and went home, to sleep. Tomorrow, so I thought, Nanette would undoubtedly resurface. On the way home, I walked along the quiet side of the Mirror's Canal. I go there often. I like antiques and I like to hunt around the old stores."

"That's when you discovered the painting?"

"Yes, I couldn't believe my eyes. I couldn't understand it. It didn't make sense. My first thought was that I *had* to have that painting. This was my chance, you see. I went to the nearest phone, rang the owner and asked him to keep the painting for me. I gave him my name. He asked for it."

He paused, searched for a cigarette, but did not light it.

"As I walked back along the Mirror's Canal, to take a good look at the painting, once more, I thought how strange it was, that Staaten should have suddenly sold the painting.

Something must have happened. Something that changed his mind, suddenly, and caused him to want to get rid of the painting, at least, get it out of the house."

He played with the cigarette, started to tear it.

"After a while, I figured the best thing to do was to ask him. Why not? I went back to the phone booth, called him and asked why he had sold *Nanette*."

He dropped the demolished cigarette in an ashtray.

"Staaten wasn't even surprised," he continued. "He told me that the painting had been stolen from his house. He had discovered the theft only ten minutes earlier. Well, I told him where he could find it."

DeKok nodded slowly.

"And," he said, grinning somberly, "and after you had told everybody, after you had awakened everyone you could think of, you decided, as a sort of afterthought, to give the vaguest possible hint to the police. Just a little puzzle to keep the boys occupied."

Wielen bowed his head.

17

"Do you think Wielen will keep his word? Will he withhold the news of Nanette's murder. What about his paper? It is, after all, news," remarked Vledder.

They were walking through the inner city, on their way back from Wielen's house, to the Warmoes Street. It was still raining. The garish lights of the neon advertising was mirrored in the wet asphalt.

DeKok pulled the collar of his raincoat a little higher and pulled his old, felt hat a little deeper down over his ears.

"In exchange," he growled, "I promised him a scoop. As soon as we know who killed Nanette, he'll be the fist to know."

"But why are you so insistent that the report of her death be kept out of the papers? After all, there are already enough people who know."

"Brother Laurens?"

Vledder shrugged his shoulders.

"If he's the killer, he doesn't need to read it in the papers."

"Exactly. That's why. I'm interested in what Laurens knows. Does he already know about her death? If so, how did he know?"

"Do you consider him a suspect?"

DeKok sighed, avoiding a puddle.

"Well, not more, or less, than any other with a reasonable motive."

"Such as?"

"Broker Staaten ..."

He spoke the name so lightly, almost as an afterthought, that Vledder slowed his step.

"*Old* Staaten?"

Slowly DeKok nodded agreement.

Suddenly it started to rain harder. A veritable downpour. They were in the middle of the Dam, far from any shelter. Vledder ran from the open square to the nearest houses. On the corner of one of the streets, he fled into *The Red Lion*. He stood panting in the lobby and looked at DeKok, who approached at speed, using his strange, waddling gait. Vledder laughed. DeKok at speed was always a comic sight.

They stood in the lobby for a while and looked at the rain. Everybody seemed to have been swept from the streets by the sudden torrents of water.

DeKok shook his hat more or less dry and wiped his face with a handkerchief. Then he took Vledder by the arm.

"Come, my boy," he said shakily, "I need something against the chill in my bones. I'll treat you to coffee and cognac."

Together they entered through the revolving door.

There were few people in the bar. The detectives hung their wet coats from a peg and found a free table near the window, without any effort at all.

A near silent waiter delivered their order.

When the man had disappeared, Vledder said:

"You didn't really mean it, did you, when you said that old man Staaten had a motive for killing Nanette?"

DeKok did not answer. He could be infuriating that way. With obvious pleasure he sipped his coffee, laced with cognac.

"Have a drink first," he said jovially, "it'll do you good. People in our job need a bracer like this, now and then."

"But Staaten wanted to marry her. Why would he want to kill the woman he was planning to marry?"

DeKok took a big swallow from his coffee.

"Revenge, injured vanity. If you listened carefully to Wielen's story, you'll remember that Nanette wasn't too flattering when she spoke about Staaten. She ridiculed him, called him 'Old Mealymouth'. That shows a remarkable lack of respect for one's future husband."

He remained silent for a while, contemplating the weather outside.

"Just imagine," he said pontifically, "that Nanette had indeed agreed to marry Staaten and that later, he found out, one way or another, that the girl didn't care for him at all, at all. On the contrary, she ran around, cheated on him and ridiculed him in conversation with others. ... Certainly enough motive for a *crime passionnel.*"

Vledder looked at his mentor with admiration.

"Indeed, you're right. I hadn't thought of that possibility."

He chewed thoughtfully on his lower lip.

"But, let's say, that your reasoning is correct. With whom did Nanette cheat on him? Wielen? From the conversations we've had so far, that seems hardly a viable relationship."

DeKok shook his head.

"Not Wielen, but Pierre Popko."

Vledder looked surprised.

"Who's Pierre Popko?"

"The painter, the one who painted the somber nude. Ronald told me. He also told me that his father used to check up on Nanette."

"Check up?"

Again DeKok nodded.

"You see, as soon as the broker had decided that he was going to marry Nanette, he didn't want her to model any longer. Especially he didn't want her to model for Popko. He didn't trust the painter."

Vledder's eyes sparkled.

"But that's beautiful," he exclaimed, "just beautiful. Then we *have* solved the case, after all. Broker Staaten finds out, during one of his checkups, that Nanette cheats on him, becomes angry and kills her."

DeKok raised his hands in a repudiating gesture.

"Ho, ho," he said, laughing, "It's not that simple. You're much too hasty, again. As always you neglect, no doubt due to youthful exuberance, a few facts. Just think . . ."

Suddenly he stopped in the middle of as sentence. His gray eyes filled with a strange expression, a bit jumpy. He looked past Vledder.

"Don't turn around," he said hoarsely, "not yet. Kristel van Daalen is behind you. She's just coming through the door. She's with a man, a tall guy, with a beard."

* * *

They were outside again, on the Dam. It was still raining, but the heavy rain had stopped. People under umbrellas passed by.

Vledder pulled an injured face.

"Was that really necessary?" he asked moodily. "Was it? Dammit! Even if she had seen us, so what? It's Saturday night, you know. Look around. People do go out. There's certainly nothing strange about that. So, Kristel is out with a friend, a tall friend with a beard. So what?" He snorted audibly, displaying utter contempt. Then, unable to leave it alone, he continued:

"You're always looking for a hidden motive. You're suspicious of everything. Ridiculous. Here we are, slinking away like thieves in the night, just because you don't want Kristel to see us. Idiotic. I'm surprised you took the time to pay the check."

DeKok whistled a Christmas song through his teeth. He always whistled Christmas songs, when he whistled, regardless of the season. Not that it made any difference. Vledder's protests rolled off his back. They did not touch him. He knew exactly what bothered his pupil. The boy was thinking of Celine, of course, his girl friend. It was Saturday night, after all. Also for them. But as long as the Nanette case had not been solved ...

Suddenly he stopped, in the middle of the street, and looked at his watch. It was past nine o'clock.

"I think you should go see her, my boy," he said fatherly. "I bet she's waiting for you, am I right?"

Vledder looked suspiciously at the face of his mentor. It seemed that DeKok could read his thoughts. It was downright eery. He swallowed.

"I ... eh, I ... think so, yes."

DeKok nodded his encouragement.

"The autopsy has been scheduled for tomorrow, at ten. Please make sure that, at the very least, you're there in time to meet Doctor Rusteloos. I'll see you at the station, afterward." He gestured. "If I'm not there, the desk sergeant will know how to reach me."

He patted his pupil on the shoulder.

"Give her my best," he said in farewell.

Hesitating, Vledder stood his ground.

"And you," he asked dubiously, "what are you going to do?"

"I'm going to try to get a hold of Ronald Staaten, before the night is out."

"*Ronald* Staaten?"

"Yes."

"Why?"

DeKok smiled gently.

"Very simple. To ask him how his date with Nanette went, last Thursday evening."

* * *

"Are you home alone?"

"No, father is home, too. Come in."

Ronald Staaten led the way. Following him, DeKok walked along the long, marble corridor. Their footsteps sounded hollow and echoed against the high walls. A wide staircase led upstairs at the end of the corridor.

"Father will be surprised."

"How's that?"

"I don't think he expected visitors."

"Ah, but my visit has to do with you, not your father."

"With me?" Surprised, Ronald turned around.

"But if your father is home, anyway," nodded DeKok, "it might be a good idea that he's present when we have our little talk. Perhaps we can eliminate a number of misunderstandings."

They climbed the wide marble stairs. At the top, mounted on a black granite pedestal, DeKok saw a bronze statue of Mercury, the god of trade, an exact replica of the larger Mercury on top of the Stock Exchange.

Ronald stopped in front of a high, carved door. He hesitated. It was as if he had to overcome something, as if he had to steel himself. It lasted but an instant. Then he opened the door and entered.

"Father," he announced, "Inspector DeKok is here."

The broker rose from a large easy chair with a high back. He looked at ease and relaxed, half glasses perched on the end of his nose, dressed in a wrinkled robe with felt slippers on his feet. He looked the opposite of the dapper man-about-town.

"With . . . eh, kay-oh-kay," Staaten smiled.

DeKok nodded.

"Indeed, you remembered."

Again Staaten smiled, politely.

"Please sit down," he said with an expansive gesture. "To what do we owe the honor of your visit? Would you like something to drink? A sherry, or would you prefer something else?"

"Cognac, please."

"Ronald . . ." the voice sounded compelling, dominating, authoritative.

"Yes, dad."

Young Staaten complied immediately. He went to an intricately carved oak buffet and returned with a sparkling cognac glass and a bottle of old French cognac. DeKok recognized the label.

Ronald looked a question at him.

"Would you like me to warm the glass?"

DeKok shook his head.

185

"No need, it'll warm in the hand."

"As you like."

It sounded shy, almost scared.

DeKok's eyebrows contracted, rippled briefly. This was a far cry from the Ronald Staaten he was familiar with; not at all the young man who had reacted so spontaneously, so passionately, above all, so arrogantly. Under the penetrating eyes of his father he behaved differently. Strange, nervous, slavish, with humility. As if he was not quite himself, but a marionette, a doll with a thousand invisible cords, connected to and controlled by the stern will of the man in felt slippers.

Ronald poured.

DeKok rocked the glass in his hand and inhaled the stimulating aroma of the drink. Meanwhile his gaze roamed the room. It was tastefully decorated. Although the room was large, almost a small ballroom, and was sparingly furnished, there was a certain atmosphere of intimacy, a warm closeness, that felt comfortable.

The walls were almost completely covered with paintings of different sizes. Most were portraits, figurative paintings. As a sort of concession to the strict figurative realism of most of the paintings, he discovered two smaller works by Renoir and a number of canvasses by lesser known French impressionists.

There were apparently no gaps. The place which, somewhere, sometime, had been occupied by the somber nude, had been filled again.

The elder Staaten watched DeKok closely.

"You're interested in paintings?"

DeKok sipped from his cognac.

"In general, no, paintings in general do not interest me. Only, sometimes, if a painting is able to waken certain

186

emotions, if it appeals to my sense of life, then, only then, will I be tempted to take a closer look, to study it. But only then."

Staaten smiled.

"It's an opinion. Don't you think, Ronald, it's a point of view."

The young man had seated himself in an easy chair. Elegantly, the legs crossed, the slender hands in front of him, fingertips pressed together.

"Yes, dad," he answered softly, "it's a point of view."

He repeated it tonelessly, without any intonation, almost mechanically. DeKok looked at both men. Father and son, totally different. Nanette Bogaard had entered in both their lives. Beautiful, frivolous, fun loving and, without doubt, a little cruel.

DeKok placed his glass on a low table and gestured.

"For instance, that particular painting, the nude on the red sofa, touched me extraordinarily. Even if I had not been involved in this case, I would still have been struck by the painting, I would not have ignored it. It fascinated me from the first time I saw it. The intense sadness in the eyes, the somber impression created by the nude body, revealed, almost sterile, without life, without any temptation, or sexual overtones. It was as if the painter, subconsciously, had detected an aura of approaching doom surrounding his model, a shadow of approaching disaster which he faithfully recorded. There was a veil of death over the painting."

A long silence remained when he finished speaking. It seemed as if DeKok's words remained in the room, they did not ebb away. They mingled with the rushing of the rain, outside. An English pendulum on the mantel piece ticked eternity away.

Ronald looked pale. His hands shook. The elder Staaten moved his feet. He was the first to break the silence.

"Pierre Popko," he said in a hoarse voice, "is a gifted painter, without a doubt. But I would not go so far as to say that he has paranormal powers, he is not a psychic. I believe, Mr. DeKok, that you may have been influenced by your rich imagination. You definitely saw more in the painting than there possibly could have been."

DeKok gave him a winning smile.

"But Nanette is dead, isn't she?"

Staaten nodded.

"Ronald told me. I believe you hinted as much, during his interrogation."

"Yes, indeed, killed, murdered in a most horrible way. I'll spare you the details. That is ..." he paused for effect, "... unless you're already familiar with them ..."

It took a while before the poison had its effect. It took several seconds. Then Staaten jumped up. His fingers writhed, as if wanting to strangle something. His eyes flashed.

"What are you trying to say?"

Every fiber of DeKok's body was tense. Only that morning he had been able to witness a fraction of the irresistible strength of the broker. He remembered the painful streaks in Vledder's neck. He was alert and ready. He pointed at Ronald.

"Your son," he said accusingly, "had a date with Nanette on the day she disappeared. She's not been seen alive after that."

Staaten's face became a mask. He looked from DeKok to his son. His glance darted back and forth.

"You, Ronald?"

The young man started to tremble under the intense stare of his father. Almost imperceptible, he nodded. His mouth opened, but no sound came forth.

For just a moment DeKok feared that Staaten was about to hit his son. But the broker controlled himself.

"You . . . you had a date with Nanette?"

"Yes, dad."

"Behind my back?"

Suddenly, something seemed to snap in the young man. It seemed to DeKok as if he suddenly pulled himself away. As if he suddenly broke the thousands of snares that connected him to the will of his father. He stopped being a puppet on a string. His attitude changed. Firmly, he looked his father straight in the eyes.

"Yes," he exclaimed sharply, "behind your back! One day I went to see Nanette at *Ye Three Roses* and told her that I needed to see her, talk to her. Alone, privately. Not in your presence, because I wouldn't have felt at ease. That's what I told her. I also told her that it really was my right to discuss certain things with her if, . . . eh, if she was going to be my mother. She refused at first, laughed at me, but finally promised to see me."

DeKok intervened.

"So you made a date with Nanette and not the other way around? I mean, you took the initiative?"

Ronald looked at him, surprised.

"Yes, I . . .."

"Where was she going?"

"You mean, where were we supposed to meet?"

"Yes."

"Here, in this house."

"What did you want to discuss with her?"

The young man started to grin. Strange, joyless, with an unpleasant grimace on his face.

"I . . . eh, I didn't have anything to discuss with her. I just wanted to kill her . . . kill her . . . kill . . . kill . . ."

He kept repeating it in a hypnotic cadence.

The elder Staaten gripped his son by the shoulder and shook him violently.

"Shut your mouth," he hissed, "shut your mouth!"

Ronald hardly noticed him.

"But she didn't come," he said, wagging his head. "No, she didn't come, she didn't come at all, she didn't . . . she didn't . . ."

An idiotic smile played around his lips.

The elder Staaten let go of his son and turned to DeKok.

"When was he supposed to meet her?"

"Thursday, Thursday evening."

For a few moment the broker remained motionless, standing between his son and the Inspector. DeKok saw him think. Fast. In a fraction of seconds he inspected, rejected and considered a number of factors. Then he sat down and sighed.

"My son." he said formally, "my son did not murder Nanette. I can testify to that. I was with him all evening."

18

"What did Doctor Rusteloos have to say?"

Vledder grinned.

"He complained that we always need him during the week-end. He wanted to know if the police was aware that there were other days in the week. Or did they only know about Saturday and Sunday?"

"Was he in a bad mood?" asked DeKok, laughing.

"But no. I've really never seen him in a bad mood. After all, he knows it isn't our fault."

"How was the autopsy?"

Vledder grimaced, showing disgust.

"I'll never get used to it. It was unusually gruesome, this time. All those separate parts ..."

"What did the doctor say about the mutilations?"

Vledder took out his notebook.

"I wrote it down for you. It was rather interesting. Just a moment, here it is: *The amputations have been performed with a certain amount of professionalism. The perpetrator—as evidenced by the condition of the skeleton, the placement of the cuts in relation to the direction of muscles and attachment of tendons—must have been possessed of more than the usual amount of anatomical knowledge.*"

He closed the note book with a slap.

"What do you think of that?"

DeKok made a vague movement with his shoulders, it was not quite a shrug.

"What do you want me to think about it?"

Demonstratively, Vledder sighed.

"Just think about Brother Laurens," he cried, irritated by DeKok's apparent obtuseness. "What do you think about his 'anatomical knowledge'? Those nurses are sometimes almost as good as doctors."

DeKok nodded slowly.

"What did the good doctor say about the cause of death?"

Vledder was offended by the scant interest DeKok seemed to display.

"Strangulation," he said, grudgingly.

"Strangled?"

"Yes."

"How?"

"With a scarf, or a nylon stocking. It could have been done by hand, but because of the mutilation, that was less easily established. Doctor Rusteloos was convinced, however, that the young woman was first strangled and that the amputations happened later."

"How much later?"

"Perhaps several hours, according to the doctor."

"Where there traces of a fight, a struggle?"

Vledder shook his head.

"There were no indications of that. No visible damage to the skin, no subcutaneous bleeding, or bruising."

"Loss of urine?"

"Probably not, there was still urine in the bladder."

DeKok nodded thoughtfully.

"Excellent," he said, "really excellent. Did you ask the doctor, in view of possible drug abuse, to look out for puncture marks, or such?"

Vledder grimaced.

"If I had wanted to know all that, I would have gone to the autopsy myself."

Amazed, DeKok looked at him.

"But why? I have an excellent assistant."

Vledder showed the beginning of a smile.

"There were no puncture marks," he said with an affected voice, "that is to say, no recent puncture marks of the skin, or such indications of drug use. Of course, a toxicological investigation has not yet been completed. Satisfied?"

"More than content," laughed DeKok.

Vledder pushed his chair closer to DeKok's desk and sat down comfortably.

"I'm always glad when such an autopsy is behind me. How did it go otherwise, last night? Did you get a hold of Ronald?"

"Yes."

"And?"

"He admitted that he had made a date with Nanette. He waited for her all night, Thursday evening, but Nanette did not show up."

Vledder grinned.

"That's easy to say."

"Indeed, but his father provided an airtight alibi. He says that he can testify that Ronald didn't kill Nanette. He was with Ronald all Thursday evening."

Vledder frowned, a deep crease appeared in his forehead.

"But," he said hesitatingly, "then those two provide each other's alibi. Difficult to break."

DeKok rubbed his hands over his face.

"Father and son Staaten," he said pensively, "united, perhaps for the first time in their lives."

He stared, a bit dreamily, at nothing at all. The elbows rested on his desk, the hands under the chin. He looked, without really seeing it, at a lost fly that tripped across his desk blotter. It stopped from time to time and rubbed the front legs together. Subconsciously he followed the movements of the fly. When it finally flew away, he rose with some difficulty. He walked over to a closet in the wall and took something out. Then he shuffled over to the peg where he kept his raincoat.

"When you have recovered sufficiently from the autopsy," he said lightly mocking, "I think I'd like to hit the road again."

"Hit the road? Where do you want to go?"

"Amsterdam West, to Ox Village. They've got an apartment building there, Woodwind, Wood House, or ..."

He fished a crumpled piece of paper from his pocket and looked at some chicken scratches.

"Oh, it's *Wood's Edge*."

Vledder's face showed complete incomprehension.

"Wood's Edge, how did you find Wood's Edge?"

DeKok grinned broadly. It was his most endearing expression.

"While you were at the autopsy, I haven't exactly been doing nothing, you know. I had a long visit at the Amsterdam City Registrar's Office."

"On a Sunday? That's closed, isn't it?"

DeKok nodded.

194

"Yes, but I found a Mr. Slosser prepared to sacrifice a few hours of his Sunday to help me look up a number of things."

Confused, Vledder looked at his mentor.

"Things, what sort of things?"

"If you had been thinking clearly," said DeKok, mildly reproachful, "you wouldn't have had to ask that question. You would have known. In any case, Wood's Edge was the result. And that's where we're going."

With bent head, a bit glum after the correction, however gentle, thinking about the how and wherefore, Vledder followed his mentor out of the room.

Suddenly he saw something hanging from DeKok's hand. It was the doll, the old doll with the fixed smile and the missing leg. The doll that DeKok had picked up at the City Dump.

"What do you want with that dirty doll?"

The question had been asked. Too quick. Vledder realized it immediately. He should not have asked the question. He should have thought about it first. DeKok never did anything without a reason. Everything he did had a purpose. The doll, too, must serve a purpose.

DeKok turned around slowly. He looked at Vledder. An almost sad expression was in his eyes.

"You still don't understand, do you?"

Soberly Vledder shook his head.

"No," he said timidly, "I have to confess ..."

The old Inspector smiled.

"Just come along, my boy," he said jovially, "I'll explain everything. I promise."

* * *

195

Wood's Edge in Ox Village, in Amsterdam, West.

The outermost of a series of inviting apartment buildings, placed in a L shape among abundant greenery. Eight stories high, centrally heated and cooled, generous elevators and more than a hundred similarly shaped units per building with large living rooms, two bedrooms, a kitchen, a lobby, a bathroom and separate entrances along spacious, continuous balconies. So typical of Northern Europe. Not unlike long rows of town houses, all on top of each other, wide galleries, roofed promenades, in front of each house, instead of a street.

Vledder parked the VW Beetle behind the building. DeKok got out of the car, doll in one hand. Vledder closed the car and followed him. Together they approached the entrance.

In front of the elevators DeKok halted and took the crumpled piece of paper out of his pocket. He showed Vledder a row of numbers.

"These are the numbers," he explained, "of the units in which live families with children. Girls. Units of families with just boys I didn't include."

"You got that from the Registrar's Office?"

DeKok nodded.

"First I want to make sure that Wood's Edge is the right building."

"Oh!?"

"You see, an old doll has certain characteristics. Children played with it. They left their marks, fantasized with it, used it to play out their imagination. It gives every doll a certain individuality, after a time."

He shook his head and looked almost tenderly at the fixed smile of the doll.

"When they were tired of playing, in the evening, mother would pick up the doll and put it away. Not once, but hundreds of times."

In the round porthole of the shaft, the light of a descending elevator became visible. The doors hissed open and a number of men, women and children emerged.

A boy of about eight looked at DeKok and the doll in his hand while passing. He walked on for a few paces. Then he stood stock still, turned and came back hesitatingly. Before DeKok could enter the elevator, he spoke:

"Where did you find the doll, mister?"

The Inspector looked down at the boy. The little guy looked neat and well cared for. He wore gray slacks, a blue blazer with brass buttons and a baseball cap.

"Why?"

"That's my little sister's doll."

"So, well, well." He was shaken by the sudden success. "You see," he continued after a moment, "I would like to return the doll to your mother. I'm looking for her. Of course, I don't know which flat you live in."

The boy laughed politely.

"Ninety three, mister. Do you want me to show you where? It's on the third floor."

"Yes, please."

They entered the elevator. On the third floor the boy ran ahead of them. He left the front door of unit ninety three open.

"Mother, mother," they heard him call, "there's a man outside and he's got Elly's doll."

It took a few moments. Then a young woman appeared in the door opening. DeKok estimated her to be in her early thirties. She looked attractive, fresh, in a flowery summer dress. She looked from DeKok to Vledder. A look full of suspicion. A small blush of excitement was on her cheeks.

DeKok smiled his best smile. It was not as good as his grin, but still very winning.

"This is Elly's doll, I believe?"

"Yes, that's Bibette," nodded the woman.

"Who?"

"Bibette, that's what my daughter calls her doll. She is rather wild with it. You have to watch her all the time. If there's an open window and you give her half a chance, she throws the doll out of the window. You found the old thing in the street, I bet. To tell the truth, I haven't seen it for a few days, now."

"Since when? Can you remember?"

Her face took on a pensive expression.

"Let's see ... I think Thursday, yes, it had to be Thursday. She was still playing with it, then."

DeKok nodded encouragement.

"Excellent, really excellent." He handed her the doll. "Well, here's Bibette again. Home, safe and sound."

The woman accepted the doll and looked at it carefully.

"Where did you find it?"

DeKok hesitated. He did not want to answer that question. A bit reticent, he scratched the back of his neck.

"At the City Dump, near Canal F."

"At the Dump?"

"Indeed."

The young woman looked at him. An expression of astonishment mingled with disbelief on her face. She dropped the doll and smoothed her dress with both hands.

"How ...?" she spluttered. "How did the doll wind up there? And how did you ...?"

DeKok raised a restraining hand.

"Perhaps," he said gently, "I'll tell you, one of these days. Just one observation: Watch more than just open windows, in connection with your daughter and the doll, watch also the flap of the garbage chute in the kitchen."

He bowed in farewell.

The woman looked after them as they walked down the gallery.

"Next time," she called, "please come when my husband is home."

DeKok waved.

"Chaste people," he snarled, "here in Wood's Edge."

Vledder grinned at his mentor.

"You're loosing your touch. You've lost your charm. That's what it is. Besides, I wonder how your wife would have reacted if two guys suddenly appeared on her front door with a dirty, old doll that they found in the garbage."

DeKok did not answer.

He looked diagonally up at the numbering of the units. It took his complete attention. The last unit on the third gallery was number 105. Beyond that it ended with a bank of elevators.

"If I'm right," he murmured, "then we'll find one hundred and twenty three just above ninety three." He spoke more to himself than to Vledder. "I'm almost certain," he concluded.

Vledder shrugged his shoulders.

"Suppose you tell me first what we're after. Perhaps I can help."

"Yes, of course," DeKok nodded absent-mindedly.

When the elevator appeared, they entered and went to the next floor up. Again they walked along a gallery. DeKok in front. Suddenly he halted and Vledder read 123.

"This is where you wanted to go?"

"Yes."

"There's no name on the door."

"No."

"Who lives here?"

Vledder became a little excited. The blood rushed to his head. The mysterious behavior of DeKok started to fray his nerves.

"Dammit," he yelled, "say something. Tell me what you want."

Preoccupied, DeKok looked up.

"What I want? I want to go inside. Just inside."

Vledder sighed.

"I don't think anyone is home. Just look, all the curtains are closed."

"I figured on that, more or less," grinned DeKok.

Carefully he looked along the gallery. When he saw nobody in sight, he took a small, steel instrument from his pocket and used it to attack the lock.

Vledder looked shocked.

"Y-you c-can't do that," he stuttered, "if the occupant complains . . ."

"I don't think he will."

Carefully probing with the sensitive tips of his fingers, the gray sleuth worried the lock.

DeKok was extremely experienced in the opening of diverse types of locks. He knew all about beards and shanks, cylinders and tumblers. Years ago he had followed a personal course of instruction with a friend, a burglar, Handy Henkie. When Henkie, after his last break-in, decided to follow the narrow, but honest path of righteousness, he had turned his complete instrumentarium over to DeKok. A melancholy offering on the altar of virtue. On certain occasions DeKok used it discreetly.

Suddenly the door of the flat opened. He motioned for Vledder to follow him. Together they entered. Carefully DeKok closed the door behind them.

Softly, on tiptoe, they slinked forward through the small foyer.

The foyer opened into a largish living room. The light was diffused. Light penetrated only marginally through the closed curtains. But it was enough to make out their surroundings.

A combination sofa was placed roughly in the middle of the room. A large, pompous piece of furniture consisting mainly of ribbed velvet and chrome steel. Nearby, closer to the window was a large standing lamp. A few cheap paintings, of the kind bought at roadside stalls, covered the walls. To the left, on a bare sideboard they saw an ugly, green vase, filled with dried corn stalks. The interior was cold and sterile, as if a caring woman's hand had never entered the flat.

Vledder touched DeKok's elbow.

"What are we looking for?" he whispered.

DeKok shrugged.

"Just look around," he whispered back. "But be careful, don't touch anything. Leave things as they are."

"OK, boss."

DeKok gave his pupil a crushing look. He didn't like to be called 'boss' and the combination of 'OK' and 'boss' infuriated him. With his hands in his pockets he entered the kitchen. There, too, the curtains were closed. In a country where people prided themselves on their interiors and where the curtains of all but the bedrooms, where seldom, if ever closed, this was remarkable. With an experienced eye, trained to see every detail, he inspected the surroundings. The knives especially took a lot of his time.

Suddenly he heard a muffled cry. Vledder, shock and disbelief on his face, came out of one of the bedrooms.

"What's the matter!?"

Vledder swallowed, trying to control himself.

"In the bedroom," he panted hoarsely.

"What?"

"Nanette's clothes."

202

19

A dark blue skirt with matching jacket, a white lace blouse, a nylon slip, bordered with lace, a garter belt and a minuscule brassiere were spread out on the bed. Next to the bed, over the back of a chair were a pair of nylon stockings and a pair of black panties with *Wednesday* embroidered on the side. A pair of blue-white pumps were placed neatly under the chair.

For a long while the detectives looked at the tableau.

"Did you see," whispered Vledder, "that it says *Wednesday* on the panties?"

"Yes."

"But she disappeared on Thursday."

DeKok sighed.

"It doesn't mean a thing. She was still alive on Thursday. That's certain. In addition to Kristel's testimony, we also know that from Barry Wielen. He visited her, that Thursday, in *Ye Three Roses*. Besides, you may remember that I asked you once about panties with the names of the days."

"I was thinking about something completely different, then," nodded Vledder.

DeKok ignored the remark. He leaned over the bed. A few long, blonde hairs sparkled against the dark blue of the jacket. He looked at them carefully, but left them untouched. Then he walked around the bed, took one of the nylon stockings from the chair and went to the window. Carefully he pushed the curtains aside and in the brighter light looked at the fine mesh of the stocking. Vledder came closer.

"You see something?"

DeKok shook his head.

"No runs. The rest of the clothing, too, seems undamaged and spotless."

"And?"

"It can mean one of two things: Either Nanette undressed herself, or the one who undressed her had plenty of time to do it carefully. I don't know if you ever tried to take off a woman's clothes . . ." He looked preoccupied at Vledder and sighed again. "Never mind, forget it," he added to his incomplete sentence.

He walked away from the window and replaced the stocking over the back of the chair. Then he looked around thoughtfully.

"A purse is missing, I think, and some form of rain clothes. Women almost always carry a purse of some sort. As far as rain gear is concerned, it rained buckets, almost all day, last Thursday."

He rubbed his hand over his gray hair.

"I'm sure it is around here somewhere. But I also think we better not touch anything else, for the moment. We might destroy some clues."

He gestured toward Vledder.

"Go downstairs and use the radio to get hold of the desk-sergeant at Headquarters. No, wait, better use a phone booth. Everybody listens to the police band, these days, and

204

I don't want the press here. Not yet. Anyway, ask the sergeant to alert the guys from forensics, the lab and so on. Also ask for a plumber."

"A plumber?"

"Yes, a person with tools, able to open and close pipes, remove gratings, fix leaks, you know."

Astonished, Vledder looked at his mentor.

"What, . . . eh, what do you want with a plumber?"

"What do you think? To solve the case, of course, what else did you think we're working on?"

He raised a cautioning finger.

"And don't forget the Dactyloscopic Service. I'm very curious to see what sort of fingers we can find here. You see, this is an interesting apartment."

Vledder's face looked disappointed.

"Listen, DeKok," he said somberly. "I know that you're very good. An old hand on the job. OK. I'm still young and I can still learn a lot from you. OK."

His tone changed, became almost threatening.

"But I've had it with your hide-and-seek games. You tell me now, and at once, how you knew about this apartment, or I won't move another muscle."

"Oh." DeKok rubbed his chin.

"Yes!" It sounded like a challenge.

DeKok made a sad, almost comical gesture.

"Well, if you put it that way . . ."

For another instant he kept his face expressionless and then it changed into a warm, broad smile.

"You're right. You most certainly are entitled to a complete explanation. I just wanted to stimulate your imagination. That's all. That's why I was so mysterious. But believe me, it isn't mysterious at all, at all. It's no more than following up on a certain train of thought. I'll explain it as soon as you're finished calling. All right?"

"OK."

DeKok took another tour of the apartment as soon as Vledder had disappeared. In the foyer, on a peg behind the door, he found a blue plastic raincoat. On a shelf above was a dark hand bag. He took the purse to the living room and inspected the contents. The usual make-up articles, handkerchief, lipstick, mirror, powder puff. But also a Dutch passport in name of Nanette Bogaard. Further he found a small flashlight, a key ring with keys and a small, flat cardboard box, filled with glass ampules, morphine.

Vledder came back within a few minutes and knocked on the window of the living room. DeKok let him in.

"Well?"

Vledder sighed.

"It isn't going to be easy, but the *Thundering Herd* will be here shortly."

DeKok smiled. Everybody knew that it was his special name for the horde of specialists who were always called in when a murder case was being investigated. Vledder's remarks meant that the full crew would be here, photographers, finger print people, forensic experts and the like. A complete crew, not just one of the stand-by groups usually to be expected on the week-end.

"Excellent," said DeKok, "really excellent. Meanwhile I found something special, here."

He showed the raincoat and the hand bag with passport and ampules. Vledder scrutinized the items.

"Well, at least we can be sure of one thing," he said after a while, "Nanette was here, in this apartment."

DeKok nodded.

"But . . . *she left in the nude.*"

"Is this," Vledder asked, "a conclusion based solely on your observation of what we have found here, so far, the clothes and so on, or is this also a part of your particular train of thought?"

DeKok smiled.

"Both," he answered. "Look, when we found the pieces of Nanette on the Dump, I was faced with a puzzle. Why, so I asked, those horrible mutilations? Why was the body cut in pieces? I just couldn't find a reasonable explanation for it. It seemed so senseless. In crimes, mutilations after death, are certainly not unheard of, but they usually have some sort of purpose. A twisted and criminal purpose, but a purpose nevertheless. Just think about the Case Kameda, that Japanese suitcase murder of a few years back. We found just the torso and the arms in the suitcase. The head, the legs and the hands were missing. Obviously, we concluded, that was to make it more difficult to identify the victim. As you know, head and hands are, with people, practically the only sure methods of identification. We don't have a brand, or a logo. With just a torso, a leg, or an arm, it is almost impossible to determine the identification with any degree of confidence. The head, on the contrary, offers all sorts of methods for identification. Just think about the eyes, the mouth, the hair, the shape of the nose, the teeth. Hands, too, are characteristic, especially because of the fingers and the finger prints."

DeKok was in "orator mode."

"In addition to obscuring the identity of the victim," he continued animated, "mutilations are also sometimes used in order to dispose of the corpse. There, too, we have numerous examples in the history of crime. I name just, by way of example, the infamous French woman-killer Landru, who more than likely first strangled his victims and then burned them. Without amputations that would have been impossible. His coal burning stove was not very big."

"A nice man, this Mr. Landru," laughed Vledder.

"Indeed, but I digress. We're not dealing with the Case Landru, but with the Case Nanette. What struck me as incongruous when we found the parts, was that there was nothing missing. Head, torso, hands, it was all there. It was also found relatively close together. Therefore the mutilations had not been performed in order to hide the identity of the victim."

He moved a little deeper into the cushions of the sofa.

"But what was the purpose? It remained a puzzle. Even when the man at the dump, . . . eh, Boer, Claus Boer, told me that the garbage in which the parts were found, came from Amsterdam West, I didn't make the connection. I could not explain the mutilations. It caused me a few extra gray hairs, I can tell you."

He smiled.

"Until . . . until *West* suddenly became important. Something clicked! I remembered the suburbs there, from before, that became absorbed within the city and the new developments, usually all apartment buildings, were formed into small villages of their own. With names like Ditch Canal, Mill Lake, Ox Village, Halfway, you name it. Then, to make it harder, or easier, depending on your point of view, some of the original names were replaced with new ones and even the individual buildings were given names. Especially in Mill Lake and Ox Village they've been building these residential barracks seemingly with assembly line methods. Anyway, all these new buildings are equipped with an individual garbage chute, covered with an airtight flap, in the kitchen. Whatever the resident wants to get rid off, hop, into the chute and large containers below the building catch and gather it all. Then comes the truck from the Sanitation Department, picks up the containers, dumps them into the truck and away we go."

"I understand," exclaimed Vledder, "of course, the chute! The murderer got rid of the corpse by means of the chute and that, naturally, could only have been done in pieces. The chutes aren't all *that* big."

"Indeed," nodded DeKok. "With a heavy-set person that would have been impossible, the parts would have had to be smaller, yet. But Nanette was just a chit of a girl. Not big at all, at all."

He became silent. Lost in thought. It was as if he saw it happen, as if he had been there, detailed images in a fleeting flash-back. Only after several minutes did he continue:

"There remained, of course, the questions: which building, what flat, which chute. In short, where exactly was Nanette Bogaard killed?"

He pulled his lower lip over his upper lip.

"With those questions I met the inestimable Mr. Slosser of the Registrar's Office. I used as my point of departure the names of the people we have so far met and about whom something was known. The question was if any of these names could be connected with an apartment building in Amsterdam West."

He used his pinky to rub the bridge of his nose.

"At first it seemed hopeless," he went on. "The name Laurens, in all possible spellings, offered no connection. I'd put the brother at the top of my list, because of his supposed anatomical knowledge. But, probably because we still don't know if it is a first name, or a surname, there was no connection. It did appear, however, that Nanette, before she went to live over *Ye Three Roses*, had never been registered in Amsterdam. From that I concluded that Brother Laurens might also not be registered in the City. After all, Nanette had met the brother in her capacity as nurse, I thought, thus *before* her arrival in Amsterdam."

"Excellent," admired Vledder, "really excellent." Neither he, nor DeKok noticed his use of one of DeKok's favorite phrases.

"Barry Wielen," continued DeKok, ignoring the interruption, "appeared to be a bit of a butterfly. He had lived at a number of addresses in Amsterdam, but never in West. I was beginning to think that we would be wasting an entire Sunday in the files, all for nothing. Then suddenly, old man Slosser discovered that the elder Staaten wasn't registered at the Emperor's Canal at all, at all, but that his address was recorded as Wood's Edge 123."

Startled, Vledder looked up.

"This flat," he said.

DeKok nodded.

"I almost couldn't believe it myself. Therefore my theatrics with the doll. When I picked that old thing up, at the dump, I really had no ulterior motive. It was more a whim, a sentimental impulse from an old man who, somewhere, saw a connection between the old, discarded doll and the young girl who had been so brutally murdered. Only later I realized that the doll had been found in the same area as the body parts. Therefore, the doll and the remains of Nanette could have been dumped by the same truck."

"I understand. So when that little boy and the woman both recognized Bibette, you knew that the remains of Nanette had to come from this building, as well."

"That's so," nodded DeKok.

"So, old man Staaten killed Nanette, after all."

DeKok rubbed his hand over his face.

"I . . . eh, I don't think so."

"What!?"

"I don't think that Staaten killed Nanette."

Totally confused, Vledder looked at his mentor.

"But this is *his* apartment! He's registered at this address."

"Registered, yes. But that doesn't necessarily mean that he lives here. The elder Staaten is a man with a refined taste, a connoisseur. He loves atmosphere, coziness, intimacy. He surrounds himself with beautiful things, paintings, handsome and comfortable furniture. Just look around you: a barely furnished apartment, without sphere, without personality, tastelessly decorated. More like a hotel room. No surroundings for the elder Staaten. He would . . ."

Suddenly DeKok stopped talking.

"What's the matter?" whispered Vledder.

"Listen, somebody at the door."

"The *herd*?"

"Too soon, no, they can't be . . ."

They rose as one and inched toward the foyer door. They could clearly hear the front door being opened. Seconds later they stood nose to nose with a man. It was Vledder's fault. He opened the living room door a little too soon.

As soon as the man spotted the detectives, he reacted immediately. In a flash he turned and ran from the flat.

"The beard!" yelled DeKok, "The beard from *The Red Lion* Catch him!"

Vledder started after the man.

20

The bearded man ran along the balconies. His long legs in a floppy pair of pants moved at incredible speed. The pale jacket, hanging loose, flapped like the wings of a bat. He did not look around.

Vledder followed, savage, determined. He was furious with himself because he gave the game away, too soon, back at the apartment. He had been too aggressive, too greedy. Thus the man had gained just enough time to make his escape. He ran on.

The sudden exertion made him pant heavily. He felt his heart. It thumbed in his chest like a steam hammer. The man with the beard fled before him. The distance between him and his quarry increased steadily.

At the end of the gallery the man shot into the elevator lobby. He realized in a flash that it would be madness to wait for an elevator. He ran to the top of the stairs.

But as he passed the bank of elevators on the floor below, aiming for the next set of stairs, one of the elevator doors opened. A few women and children emerged. Unaware of the situation.

They formed a sudden obstacle for the bearded man. They were too close. He could not avoid them. His speed was too great.

Right in front of him was a little girl, perhaps six years old, or less, with a doll in her arms. In a desperate attempt to avoid the child, he jumped. It was a wild, uncalculated jump and he lost control. His left foot slipped, found no traction and with a sickening thud he fell on the granite floor.

Dazed, he remained down. Almost unconscious. From a distance he heard women and children scream. It was a strange, thrilling sound of people in panic. He opened his eyes and looked for the source. He could not see very well. The images at a distance were blurred. Closer, it was better. Next to his head was a doll. He could make out the shape and the features. It was an old, plastic doll with a fixed smile. It fascinated him no end. He did not know why. He could not tear his eyes away from that fixed, soulless smile. He was still looking at it when he lost consciousness completely.

* * *

"What was the verdict, at the hospital?"

Vledder sighed.

"He's in shock. For the time being we're not allowed to ask him any questions."

"Serious?"

"No, not exactly. The doctor thought that he would be all right, in a few days. In retrospect it wasn't all that bad."

"And the little girl?"

"Nothing, a few scrapes and bruises on arms and legs. Her mother took her home already."

"I'm glad about that," said DeKok, relieved.

Vledder bit on his lower lip.

"Me too, believe me. I really feel a bit responsible for that tumble, you know. I should never have given Pierre a chance to run away. If I had just let him enter all the way, we would have had him. But that guy was so fast."

"I hope," grinned DeKok, "you arranged for surveillance in the hospital."

"Of course, what do you think? I managed to convince the Commissaris to assign two constables. One in the corridor and the other one next to the bed."

"What about the windows?"

Vledder shook his head wearily.

"No problem. The windows look out on a closed courtyard, no escape."

DeKok rose from his chair.

"Excellent," he said. "Really excellent. Two constables seems more than enough, then. I wouldn't want to lose our friend at this late date, you see."

"Yes, I can understand that. You worked hard enough to get a hold of him. Have you heard anything yet, from the technical services?"

Slowly DeKok nodded.

"Yes, just before you came back from the hospital, I talked with Doctor Beskes, from the lab. He told me that they'd found blonde hair on the sides of the garbage chute and in the grating of the drainpipe in the shower. They also found clear evidence of human tissue. An overwhelming indication for my theory that Nanette was killed and dismembered inside the flat."

"And what about prints?" asked Vledder, while nodding agreement with DeKok's statement.

"Well, they found prints all over the place, a great many of them. In the kitchen, the bathroom, everywhere. But it's too soon to tell. They have to be compared and correlated."

"What do you think?"

"I think they'll match."

Vledder looked at him probingly.

"You mean, that . . . eh, the prints will probably belong to Pierre Popko and Nanette?"

"Yes."

Vledder shook his head and sighed.

"To be completely honest, I don't understand a thing. How, for instance, did those two get to use the apartment belonging to Staaten? And why the murder? What motive did Popko have to kill Nanette? I can't see it. Really, I can't see it."

With hands deeply buried in his pockets, DeKok began to pace up and down the large detective room. Slowly his feet shuffled over the worn linoleum. Despite his success, so far, he was depressed and discouraged.

He halted in front of the window. The rain hid the rooftops across the street in a nebulous veil.

"Cats and dogs," he murmured, "dog days."

Suddenly he thought about his old mother and her superstitious fear of those days in July. Responsive to the tender feelings it invoked, he smiled softly to himself. He saw the so familiar face before his mind's eye: Two sparkling eyes in a lovely face full of dear wrinkles. 'Careful, my boy,' he heard her say, 'the dog days of summer can be dangerous . . . dangerous . . . danger . . .' Her voice echoed in his brain.

For a while longer, he remained motionless in front of the window, trying to come to a decision. Then he turned, took his hat and coat in passing and waddled out of the office.

"Come," he called from the door, "we're going to the hospital. I want that painter's story now, today!"

Vledder looked at him in astonishment.

"But," he called after him, "What about the doctor . . . ?"

216

DeKok ignored him. Unperturbed he walked on. Vledder followed him, shaking his head, the raincoat in a bunch on his shoulder.

* * *

DeKok could never really get used to it. The typical smell of a hospital, that combination of lysol, carbolic soap and other, unidentifiable odors. Whenever he had to visit a hospital, in the course of his profession, he made his stay as short as possible.

"Where's he?" he nudged Vledder.

"Upstairs, second floor."

They climbed the stairs. A couple of young nurses, darted past them. Vledder showed his most pleasant face and a beaming smile. DeKok did not exert himself.

They found a young constable in the corridor on the second floor. He stood in front of a door, legs wide apart.

DeKok grinned at him in a friendly sort of way.

"I'm Inspector DeKok."

"Yessir, with kay-oh-kay, I've seen you before," laughed the constable.

"Excellent, really excellent. Where's your partner?"

"Inside. Holding the suspect's hand, I expect."

"Excellent," repeated DeKok grinning, "really excellent. Just call him out here, will you? Vledder and I will take over for a while. Look around, get a cup of coffee, pinch the nurse, whatever. Be back here in about half an hour."

"Half an hour?" grimaced the constable.

"Yes, about that. And don't worry about him, in the meantime. We'll take good care of him and we won't leave before you're back."

217

The young constable nodded. He opened the door of the room and motioned for his partner, a big, dark, muscular man who was sitting next to the bed, a bit embarrassed, to come outside.

"Come, sister of mercy," he joked, "the detectives will take over, for a while."

His partner rose gratefully from the chair. Any interruption of the boring assignment was welcome. His large face beaming, he left the room.

As soon as the constable had left the room, Vledder and DeKok approached the bed. They stood at the foot end of the bed and looked at the man who had surprised them in the apartment. A renewed confrontation.

* * *

Pierre Popko looked pale. He was on his back, bandages, like a turban, around his head. He looked calmly at his visitors. The blue eyes were clear.

DeKok took his old, felt hat from his head and kept it awkwardly, a bit shyly, in front of his chest. It was an uncomfortable gesture, as if he did not really know what to do with it.

Vledder looked at him from the side. DeKok irritated him, at such moments. The shy, forced bashfulness of his mentor exasperated him no end. It was nothing but a pose, an act, Vledder knew that, it was designed to keep his opponents off guard. It was just so evident, so transparent, that Vledder could simply not understand how anybody could be fooled by it.

"How are you?" he heard him ask. It sounded worried.

Pierre Popko gave a wan smile.

218

"Not too bad, yes, not too bad." Carefully he felt for the bandages on his head. "My head still hurts."

DeKok pushed a chair closer to the head end of the bed and sat down.

"Well, that was quite a fall you took."

The painter tried to grin.

"Yes," he said with a grimace, "you might say that. How ... eh, how's the child?"

"All right, a few scrapes and bruises. Nothing serious. Home already."

"I tried to avoid her." The hand on the white sheet made a helpless movement. "But I couldn't. I was going rather fast and the descent of the stairs increased my speed too much. I was too close, too fast."

Silence fell over the room.

Vledder walked away from the foot of the bed. He went to the window and sat down on a short bench, took out his notebook and poised himself to take notes. He knew this was just the preliminary skirmish. Before long, DeKok would steer the conversation in the direction of the murder. He knew his mentor so well. That was part of his tactic. He would approach the subject in which he was interested, calmly, obliquely, sideways, almost unnoticed. Carefully the painter turned his head, it obviously was painful for him to do so.

"You're Inspector DeKok, aren't you?"

"You know me?" asked DeKok, nodding agreement.

"Kristel told me," answered the painter after a slight hesitation.

"You know Kristel?"

"Kristel is an old friend," smiled the painter.

"*Old* friend?"

"As a friend, yes. I've known her since before she started *Ye Three Roses* in Duke Street. I met her through her brother."

"Frank Bogaard?"

"Yes, indeed, that's what he called himself. For one reason or another he assumed his mother's name as a pen name. His real name is Frank van Daalen. Frank wrote a number of interesting books. I liked his work. One night, in some bar, somebody introduced us. It was the beginning of a short friendship."

"What happened to him?"

Pierre Popko made a slight, almost imperceptible movement with his shoulders.

"I don't know. As I said, our friendship didn't last all that long. He hung around with people I didn't care for. It resulted in a rift, eventually. Later, I heard that he might have been hooked on drugs. I don't know if it's true, or not. I just lost touch."

DeKok nodded.

"But . . . eh, your friendship with Kristel survived?"

Popko showed some discomfort, for the first time since they had entered. The question seemed to worry him.

"Well?" pressed DeKok.

"My . . . eh, my friendship with Kristel survived."

His voice sounded suddenly sharper.

The detective leaned closer.

"And when Nanette disappeared . . .?"

As casually as possible he posed the question. Like a hawk he looked for a reaction.

A slight blush colored the face of the painter.

"That . . . that's something else. That had nothing to do with Kristel and me. I mean, that was outside our friendship. Kristel understood that."

"I don't." DeKok shook his head.

"What?"

"I don't understand it."

Pierre Popko sighed deeply.

"Nanette, Nanette was a drug, perhaps, in retrospect I should call it a disease, an aberration." He spread his arms wide. "She loved me, she said, she loved only me."

He shook his head and closed his eyes tightly. His body shook. His lips trembled above his beard. His hands crumpled the sheets.

"The snake," he hissed. "The viper. Believe me, I went through hell, the last few days." He sighed, overcome with some emotion, it sounded like a sob. "But I have been cleansed, cleansed ..."

DeKok felt the painter's face with the back of his hand. The face was hot. He feared a renewed shock. After all, this interrogation had been prohibited by the attending physician. He did not have permission. If something happened ...

"Let's discuss this calmly," he said softly, soothingly. "Calmly, like reasonable people. It'll do you good, believe me. It clears the air. It's a relief. You ... eh, you *do* want to talk about it, don't you?"

Pierre nodded weakly.

DeKok took the sheet and used a tip to carefully wipe the sharp nose, the corners of the eyes and the cheeks. The painter's face was bathed in sweat. Drops of sweat beaded his beard.

"When you visited your old friend Kristel in *Ye Three Roses*, you met Nanette there?"

"Yes."

"It was the first time you had met her?"

"Yes."

"You found her attractive?"

"Yes."

"You fell in love?"

"Not immediately."

DeKok paused. He smiled encouragingly at the painter. Pierre had become a lot calmer. The friendly, softly insistent voice of DeKok had calmed him. He did not shake anymore.

"What happened next?"

"Nanette was so different from Kristel. More outgoing, more frivolous. When she found out that I painted, she forced herself on me, persistent, shameless. She wanted to come to the studio and offered to model for me."

Softly he grinned to himself.

"At first I refused. Really. I didn't want to get involved. You see, actually I was afraid of her. She confused me. Whenever she was with me, I felt uncertain, not sure of myself, restless. It was as if I didn't exist anymore, as if the essential 'me' had ceased to exist. You understand? I wasn't myself anymore. I became a creature without a will of my own."

He remained silent for a while.

"One night she told me that she loved me."

He covered his face with both hands.

"From then on, everything went wrong."

"How's that?"

Popko licked his dry lips.

"She told me that she would make me famous. A great painter. Painting, she said, was more than a matter of just talent, or art, it was even more a matter of publicity. It didn't matter too much what you painted, as long as people talked about it. She told me she knew a reporter and that she could convince him to write a number of articles about me."

Again he smiled wanly, swallowed and then continued:

222

"It sounded too good to be true. You must keep in mind that I'd never been very successful with my paintings. I live in poverty, really, in an old barn on Prince's Island. I call it my studio, but it's little more than a shack, a playground for rats, at night. Once, when I showed Staaten how the rats had been gnawing on my paints, he gave me the key to his flat in Wood's Edge. I was allowed to use the flat as a bedroom."

He rubbed the back of his hands over his dry lips.

"I used to take Nanette there, from time to time. Whenever she was with me, I'd live in a sort of dream, almost a drunken stupor. I felt like I walked on air. Wings on both feet."

DeKok nodded understanding.

"How did Nanette meet Staaten?"

"Through me. I'd told her about Staaten. Told her the apartment belonged to him. Told her he was a rich man with a fantastic collection of paintings. I told her that he sometimes gave me a commission."

He took a deep breath. Talking seemed to become easier.

"She pressed me," he continued, "to introduce her to him. She wanted to meet him. She would then, in her own way, take care that Staaten would give me important projects."

"And that's how you received the commission for the nude on the sofa."

"That painting was not a commission." He shook his head.

"What?"

"But no, it was just another of Nanette's ideas. Let's show old man Staaten what I look like, she said, the more he sees, the more curious he'll be, she thought."

"And what about the red sofa?"

"That was another of her ideas. Once, in a sentimental mood, Staaten had told her about his wife. Nanette was a good listener, when she wanted to be. She knew that the red sofa was a favorite of the late Mrs. Staaten."

Pierre Popko swallowed.

"She wanted to get old Staaten crazy enough, so he would ask her to marry him."

"And you were enlisted to help her?"

"Yes, that's what she said. I made a few nice sketches of her, pretty realistic, almost provocative. I showed them to Staaten. He was all shook up about them."

"But how could you do that? She loved you, she said. And you were supposed to help her trap the old man, Staaten. That, that's almost incomprehensible."

Again Pierre buried his face in his hands.

"I don't know. I don't know any more."

There was despair in his voice.

"She talked about a marriage of convenience. It didn't mean anything and it wouldn't affect our relationship in the least. On the contrary, it would bind us closer together. A marriage with a rich man would also afford her the opportunity to do a lot for me, professionally. And as soon as Staaten died, there would be plenty of years left."

He moved his head from side to side.

"I don't know. I really don't know anymore. I was simply drugged, mesmerized, apathetic. It was as if I had lost every form of judgement."

"When did you again regain your senses?" asked DeKok, watching him closely.

Popko pressed himself into a sitting position. He sat straight up in bed and bent his head backward. His mouth was partially open. It was if he stretched himself after a long and deep sleep.

224

"I finally woke up," he said softly, "when I saw her dead in front of me. It was as if I had been wakened from a nightmare. It was all so unreal. Her death, too. When I finally realized that, I cried over her corpse. A long, long time. So long that I had no tears left."

"And then?"

The painter slid back down in the bed. He rested his head on the pillow and stared at the ceiling.

"Suddenly," he went on, "I realized that she had to disappear. That she couldn't remain in the apartment. That was impossible. It was unthinkable. If they'd found her . . . After all, Staaten knew I used the flat. I panicked. In a wild, unthinking impulse I lifted her on my shoulder and walked out, onto the gallery. There's an emergency staircase that almost nobody ever uses."

He paused again, lost in memories.

"I was almost downstairs, when a car stopped at the bottom and somebody came up the stairs. My heart shot in my throat, I can tell you. As fast as possible, I turned around and quickly went up the stairs. It was easy. Nanette wasn't heavy. I saw a number of cars and bicycles on the road behind the building. Suddenly I realized that I could be seen from everywhere. Anybody could see me. I got scared. I started to run with the corpse over my shoulder, as fast as I could. I became more and more scared. I heard sounds that weren't there. I saw doors open that were closed. It was hell, complete hell. I think I'd lost my mind when I finally got her back in the flat."

The painter stopped talking, rubbed his hands over his face, his beard. Sweat poured out of him.

"On the sofa, on the sofa in the living room, I thought about a way to get rid of her."

"That's when you thought about the garbage chute?"

He nodded slowly in reply.

"Slowly a strange calm came over me. A resigned calm. Never before in my life do I remember ever having been that calm. Carefully I undressed her and when she was naked, I carried her to the bathroom and lowered her in the shower stall."

"That's where it happened?"

"Yes, that's where it happened," he answered with a sigh.

DeKok fell back against the support of the chair. He felt torpid, tired. The interrogation of the painter had exhausted him.

He thought about the conversation and let every word pass in review. He had an uncanny knack for doing that. It was as if a tape-recorder played back the entire conversation. Every word, every intonation, every expression, every detail was once more examined. He checked to see if he had everything, enough to satisfy the District Attorney, the Judge-Advocate, the Courts and . . . the Defense.

He looked at his watch. More than half an hour had passed. The constables had not yet returned. Idly he wondered where they had gone.

Suddenly he remembered something. Something vital. A question he had not yet asked. He looked at the painter.

"But what was the motive? I mean, what was the immediate cause, what triggered you to kill her?"

Popko's eyes opened wide. His face showed nothing but utter amazement.

"Kill her?"

"Yes."

"But I, . . . eh, I *didn't* kill her."

"What!?"

"I didn't kill her. Nanette was already dead, when I found her."

DeKok swallowed in total astonishment. Never before, in his long career, had an answer shocked him so. It was as if the room started to spin around him. As if the floor had disappeared from underneath his chair. He pressed his eyes closed to shut himself off from the turmoil around him. From a distance he heard Vledder move.

The door of the room opened. Both constables were visible in the opening.

"Sorry," said the younger of the two, "it took a little longer than expected. When we finally found the kitchen the coffee wasn't ready."

Weakly DeKok rose.

"Never mind," he said groggily.

He picked up his old, felt hat from the bed, murmured a hasty farewell and waddled into the corridor.

Vledder looked after him from the door opening. His face was serious and distraught. He felt instinctively that it would be better not to follow his partner, this time. He had to leave him alone. He had to take the next step by himself, without Vledder. It was his mission, his job, his duty.

* * *

The belt had been twisted so often that it resembled a rope. DeKok pulled it a little tighter around his old raincoat and pressed his fists deeper into the pockets. Slowly he strolled away from the hospital, across a number of bridges, along canals, oblivious to his surroundings. A surly, gruff look clouded his face. Every once in a while he used a handkerchief to wipe the rain from his face. It did not slow him down. In his typical, somewhat rolling, waddling gait he walked on, past the ferries, across the Dam. There were times when he hated his profession, when he would rather be anything else, except a detective. At those times he hated the Law, hated Justice. This was one of those moments.

He walked the length of a number of streets and then turned the corner of Duke Street. In front of *Ye Three Roses* he halted and looked up at the old, cast-iron sign over the door. It had been decorated with a shield, a coat of arms. He saw it for the first time. *Three red roses on a white field*.

He looked at it for a long time, contemplated leaving, to just walk away. But he knew at the same time that it would be useless, senseless.

He placed a finger on the buzzer and pushed.

21

Vledder had not forgotten the invitation of his mentor, partner and friend. A week later, on a Sunday, he and Celine had come visiting. Mrs. DeKok had, as promised, made a special effort to make it a festive occasion. A small, intimate party. Later that evening they were comfortably gathered in the living room.

Celine appeared to be a darling of a girl, a young woman, corrected DeKok in silence. He admired the good sense and taste of his pupil. At first Celine had been a bit withdrawn, a bit shy, but eventually she participated cheerfully in the conversation.

When there was a gap in the conversation, Celine said unexpectedly: "So, Kristel van Daalen killed Nanette?"

"Why the sudden interest?" asked DeKok perplexed.

She laughed, a bit shyly.

"I lived through that time with you, in a sense. When we were together, I helped Dick to think, didn't I, Dick?"

Vledder grinned, a bit embarrassed.

"Yes," he swallowed, "she helped think."

"Well, what was the result?"

She smiled a sunny smile.

"I would never have thought of Kristel. Actually, she was the one I least suspected."

The gray sleuth pushed his lower lip forward.

"Did Dick tell you everything? How we surprised Brother Laurens at the funeral? How we arrested him? How ..."

"Yes," interrupted Celine, "I know all that, but you dealt with Kristel on your own."

DeKok sighed.

"Kristel, yes, Kristel."

He paused to order his thoughts.

"After Pierre Popko," he began hesitatingly, "told me, in the hospital, that he hadn't killed Nanette, but that he had found her already dead, I suddenly realized the true chain of events. Kristel was responsible for the death of Nanette. It was just an additional confirmation that her finger prints were found in the flat, later, by the experts."

He took a sip from his cognac, his favorite beverage.

"Kristel," he continued, "knew about the flat in Wood's Edge. She had known for some time. Long before Nanette came to spoil the idyll, she and Pierre used to meet each other there. Just like Nanette, she had a key to the apartment. That Thursday, just after Nanette had left, Pierre stopped by *Ye Three Roses* to tell her that he would be at the flat a little later than usual. He was working on something in his studio that he wanted to finish. He asked Kristel to pass the message on to Nanette. Kristel promised to do so. She didn't tell him that Nanette had already left. It seemed like a unique opportunity to her. So, she went to the apartment, after closing time, and let herself in with her key. After a short, but intense exchange of words, she strangled Nanette. Kristel has strong hands. She's been playing tennis for years. At least three, four times a week."

"But why?" asked Celine, making an impatient gesture.

DeKok sighed a deep sigh and took another sip from his drink.

"Well, you see, despite everything, I feel a deep sympathy for Kristel. Not just because she is an extremely beautiful woman. Kristel loved Pierre Popko. She had been in love with him for a long time. When Nanette appeared she relinquished her love. Reluctantly she let go of her lover. It was a constant source of sorrow and regret. But she couldn't fight Nanette. Nanette had an almost magical influence over men. She could have any man she wanted, just by snapping her fingers. Kristel could only hope that Pierre would get over his infatuation, that he would wake up and that he would come back to her."

They listened to him with bated breath. After a short hesitation, he went on:

"When Nanette revealed her plans to marry Staaten, Pierre lost his head. He confided in Kristel and told her about Nanette's plans and aspirations. Kristel was furious. This, more than anything else, was so contrary to her own sense of rightness, her own morals, that she called Nanette to account."

He remained silent for a moment.

"That's when Nanette threatened her."

Celine looked at DeKok with wide eyes.

"Nanette threatened her?"

"Yes, Nanette threatened Kristel. It became her death sentence. She told Kristel that if she, Kristel, were to interfere in any way at all, if she so much as tried to stop her, she would get Pierre hooked on drugs, she would make him into the same sort of vegetable as she had done to Frank."

"Morphine!" gasped Celine.

"Yes, morphine."

Celine's eyes flashed in anger.

"What a snake," she hissed.

A blush of complete indignation colored her cheeks.

DeKok smiled sadly.

"Yes," he said, "a snake in the shape of an angel."

About the Author:

Albert Cornelis Baantjer (BAANTJER) is the most widely read author in the Netherlands. In a country with less than 15 million inhabitants he sold, in 1988, his millionth "DeKok" book. Todate more than 35 titles in his "DeKok" series have been written and more than 2.5 million copies have been sold. Baantjer can safely be considered a publishing phenomenon. In addition he has written other fiction and non-fiction and writes a daily column for a Dutch newspaper. It is for his "DeKok" books, however, that he is best known. *Every* year more than 70,000 Dutch people check a "Baantjer/DeKok" out of a library. The Dutch version of the Reader's Digest Condensed Books (called "Best Books" in Holland) has selected a Baantjer/DeKok book five (5) times for inclusion in its series of condensed books.

Baantjer writes about Detective-Inspector DeKok of the Amsterdam Municipal Police (Homicide). Baantjer is himself an ex-inspector of the Amsterdam Police and is able to give his fictional characters the depth and the personality of real characters encountered during his long police career. Many people in Holland sometimes confuse real-life Baantjer with fictional DeKok. The author has never before been translated.

This author is a proven best-seller and the careful, authorized translations of his work, published by New Amsterdam Publishing should fascinate the English speaking world as it has the Dutch reading public.

DeKok and Murder on the Menu
Baantjer

On the back of a menu from the Amsterdam Hotel-Restaurant *De Poort van Eden* (Eden's Gate) is found the complete, signed confession of a murder. The perpetrator confesses to the killing of a named blackmailer. Inspector DeKok (Amsterdam Municipal Police, Homicide) and his assistant, Vledder, gain possession of the menu. They remember the unsolved murder of a man whose corpse, with three bullet holes in the chest, was found floating in the waters of the Prince's Canal. A year-old case which was almost immediately turned over to the Narcotics Division. At the time it was considered to be just one more gang-related incident. DeKok and Vledder follow the trail of the menu and soon more victims are found and DeKok and Vledder are in deadly danger themselves. Although the murder was committed in Amsterdam, the case brings them to Rotterdam and other, well-known Dutch cities such as Edam and Maastricht.

First American edition of this European Best-Seller.

ISBN 1 881164 31 4

Murder in Amsterdam
Baantjer

The two very first "DeKok" stories for the first time in a single volume. In these stories DeKok meets Vledder, his invaluable assistant, for the first time. The book contains two complete novels. In *DeKok and the Sunday Strangler*, DeKok is recalled from his vacation in the provinces and tasked to find the murderer of a prostitute. The young, "scientific" detectives are stumped. A second murder occurs, again on Sunday and under the same circumstances. No sign of a struggle, or any other kind of resistance. Because of a circumstantial meeting, with a "missionary" to the Red Light District, DeKok discovers how the murderer thinks. At the last moment DeKok is able to prevent a third murder. In *DeKok and the Corpse on Christmas Eve*, a patrolling constable notices a corpse floating in the Gentlemen's Canal. Autopsy reveals that she has been strangled and that she was pregnant. "Silent witnesses" from the purse of the murdered girl point to two men who played an important role in her life. The fiancee could not possibly have committed the murder, but who is the second man? In order to preserve his Christmas Holiday, DeKok wants to solve the case quickly.

**First American edition of these European
Best-Sellers in a single volume.**

ISBN 1 881164 00 4

DeKok and the Dead Harlequin
Baantjer

Murder, double murder, is committed in a well-known Amsterdam hotel. During a nightly conversation with the murderer DeKok tries everything possible to prevent the murderer from giving himself up to the police. Risking the anger of superiors DeKok disappears in order to prevent the perpetrator from being found. But he is found, thanks to a six-year old girl who causes untold misery for her family by refusing to sleep. A respected citizen, head of an important Accounting Office is deadly serious when he asks for information from the police. He is planning to commit murder. He decides that DeKok, as an expert, is the best possible source to teach him how to commit the perfect crime.

First American edition of this European Best-Seller.

ISBN 1 881164 04 7

DeKok and the Sorrowing Tomcat
Baantjer

Peter Geffel (Cunning Pete) had to come to a bad end. Even his Mother thought so. Still young, he dies a violent death. Somewhere in the sand dunes that help protect the low lands of the Netherlands he is found by an early jogger, a dagger protruding from his back. The local police cannot find a clue. They inform other jurisdictions via the police telex. In the normal course of events, DeKok (Homicide) receives a copy of the notification. It is the start of a new adventure for DeKok and his inseparable side-kick, Vledder. Baantjer relates the events in his usual, laconic manner.

First American edition of this European Best-Seller.

ISBN 1 881164 05 5

TENERIFE!

by Elsinck

Madrid 1989. The body of a man is found in a derelict hotel room. The body is suspended, by means of chains, from hooks in the ceiling. A gag protrudes from the mouth. He has been tortured to death. Even hardened police officers turn away, nauseated. And this won't be the only murder. Quickly the reader becomes aware of the identity of the perpetrator, but the police are faced with a complete mystery. What are the motives? It looks like revenge, but what do the victims have in common? Why does the perpetrator prefer black leather cuffs, blindfolds and whips? The hunt for the assassin leads the police to seldom frequented places in Spain and Amsterdam, including the little known world of the S&M clubs in Amsterdam's Red Light District. In this spine-tingling thriller the reader follows the hunters, as well as the hunted and Elsinck succeeds in creating near unendurable suspense.

First American edition of this European Best-Seller.

ISBN 1 881164 51 9

From critical reviews of **Tenerife!**:

... A wonderful plot, well written—Strong first effort—Promising debut—A successful first effort. A find!—A well written book, holds promise for the future of this author—A first effort to make dreams come true—A jewel of a thriller!—An excellent book, gripping, suspenseful and extremely well written ...

MURDER BY FAX

by Elsinck

Elsinck's second effort consists entirely of a series of Fax copies. An important businessman receives a fax from an organization calling itself "The Radical People's Front for Africa". It demands a contribution of $5 million to aid the struggle of the black population in South Africa. The reader follows the alleged motives and criminal goals of the so-called organization via a series of approximately 200 fax messages between various companies, police departments and other persons. All communication is by Fax and it will lead, eventually, to kidnapping and murder. Because of the unique structure, the book's tension is maintained from the first to the last fax. The reader also experiences the vicarious thrill of "reading someone else's mail". After his successful first book, *Tenerife!*, Elsinck now builds an engrossing and frightening picture of the uses and mis-uses of modern communication methods.

First American edition of this European Best-Seller.

ISBN 1 881164 52 7

From critical reviews of **Murder by Fax**:

... Riveting — Sustains tension and is totally believable — An original idea, well executed — Unorthodox — Engrossing and frightening — Well conceived, written and executed — Elsinck sustains his reputation as a major new writer of thrillers ...

About Elsinck:

Henk Elsink (ELSINCK) is a new star on the Dutch detective-thriller scene. His first book, "Tenerife!", received rave press reviews in the Netherlands. Among them: "A wonderful plot, well written." (De Volkskrant), "A successful first effort. A find!" (Het Parool) and "A jewel!" (Brabants Dagblad).

After a successful career as a stand-up comic and cabaretier, Elsinck retired as a star of radio, TV, stage and film and started to devote his time to the writing of books. He divides his time between Palma de Mallorca (Spain), Turkey and the Netherlands. He has written three books and a fourth is in progress.

Elsinck's books are as far-ranging as their author. His stories reach from Spain to Amsterdam, from Brunei to South America and from Italy to California. His books are genuine thrillers that will keep readers glued to the edge of their seats.

The author is a proven best-seller and the careful, authorized translations of his work, published by New Amsterdam Publishing should fascinate the English speaking world as it has the European reading public.